I0756015

FINISHING LINE PRESS
www.finishinglinepress.com

The Very Terrible Drowning of Bryan Price

a novella by

Colleen Alles

Finishing Line Press
Georgetown, Kentucky

ISBN 979-8-89990-402-8 First Edition

This novella is a work of fiction. The names, characters, and incidents in it are the work of the author's imagination. Any semblance to actual persons, living or dead, is entirely coincidental. No generative artificial intelligence (AI) was used in the writing of this work.

Publisher: Leah Huete de Maines
Editor: Christen Kincaid
Cover Art: Ben Boss
Author Photo: Chloe Farber
Cover Design: Elizabeth Maines McCleavy

Order online: www.finishinglinepress.com
also available on amazon.com

Author inquiries and mail orders:
Finishing Line Press
PO Box 1626
Georgetown, Kentucky 40324
USA

You can be of two minds about something, but not two hearts.

Marc J. Sheehan

Kate—*After*

For as long as possible, I resist the urge to blink.

It's like I believe if I manage to hold my eyes open without giving them a break—what? What do I think will happen? Do I really think the scene in front of me might change?

What is happening? What the hell just happened?

There's a sharp pain in my arm. I look down. Chelsea is clutching my elbow. Hard.

"Ouch," I say, pulling my arm away.

"Sorry," she murmurs.

She meets my eyes. I forget for a moment I'm her supervisor—that I'm nearly old enough to be her mother. Maybe. If I'd started younger. Her hazel eyes are wide. She can't believe what's happening, either.

"We need to get Luke out of here," I say.

She nods. Her face looks like a wooden spoon—curved and blank.

I look around. There are men and women everywhere—dozens of them. Kids too. Baby strollers. People with dogs on leashes. They're all looking at each other, asking each other questions—the people, not the dogs. The dogs are wagging their tails, which I know means they're engaged with the situation, not necessarily that they're happy. No one's happy right now. Everyone is pointing at the water. They're pointing at me.

What the hell just happened?

People are saying someone drowned. People are saying someone's dead.

People are looking at me.

Down by the shoreline, two men in full-body wetsuits pull something big out of the water. That something big is a body. A man. Chelsea grabs my elbow again, but this time I don't say "ouch." This time, I welcome the pain. It's proof I am alive.

There's a siren. An ambulance arrives.

Someone must have called one. Thank God. Why didn't I think to?

I watch the ambulance drive over the grass. The crowd parts. It's like the Red Sea, and the ambulance is Moses. No, that's not right. The ambulance is the group of people Moses led. They followed him. They trusted him. Why am I thinking about the Bible? Was Moses really trustworthy? I don't know if I'm supposed to hope for a miracle. People around me are murmuring things like, *Oh my God*. Some people are crying. Some people are saying we should cancel the race. Other people are asking, *how did this happen?*

People are still looking at me. People are texting. If they aren't, their hands are covering their mouths.

Chelsea isn't at my side anymore. She's rushing down to the paramedics at the water's edge. Luke is still standing there. He shouldn't be here. I'm old enough to be his mother. Sometimes at work, I feel like I am. He should listen to me.

I can't think straight. I try not blinking again.

I wish I wasn't hungover.

I wish I'd been firm with Paul last night when he poured the rest of the bottle into my glass. I *should* have been firmer. More firm? Firmer. I'd had three glasses already, maybe four. Generous pours. Okay, four. There had been a little Merlot left in the bottle. I wish I'd refused it. I wish I'd saved it instead of feeling the urge to empty the bottle. I can't drink like I used to. I keep telling my husband. He keeps acting as though I can.

"What time are you waking up tomorrow?" he'd asked.

"Five," I'd groaned.

"You'll be fine. You're a pro."

Yet I'd woken up in a fog. My brain is somewhere else. More people are crying around me. Mothers with strollers are turning to leave.

I want to tell them to take Luke. He's a baby, too—just seventeen. Same age as my twins, Krista and Keith. I'm thankful my kids aren't here. I wish Paul were here. I want to hold him responsible for my hangover, even though I know it's my fault. I want to hold his hand.

Finally, I take a deep breath and walk to Chelsea. I need to stand by her. I am the Interim Director. I am the Race Organizer. Paramedics are hunched over the man in a black wetsuit—the one they just pulled out of the water.

It's Bryan Price. There's no mistaking his face.

He used to be my husband—a long time ago. A *really* long time ago. Not Krista and Keith's dad. That's Paul. But Bryan Price and I were married, once upon a time, and now the EMT is pumping desperately at his torso, pushing in, pushing in, not taking his eyes off Bryan's chest.

He's my ex-husband, in other words.

Is he actually dead?

Around him, too, crouching at his left side, facing the water, I see a petite blonde woman. She's trying to get to his head, his face. She's reaching out with her hands. She's crying. Another EMT pulls her back, gently, touching her shoulders, carefully avoiding her belly, trying to get her to stand. I hear him tell her to give Bryan and the EMT space.

I get closer to Bryan like I'm drawn to him. It feels like a scene from a movie, but I watch the woman take a few steps toward me, even though her face is almost out of focus. For the tenth time, I wish I wasn't hungover. I'm too old to make such stupid mistakes. She's screaming at me. She screams something else. Her voice is unclear; it's like she's underwater.

Then, I make out what she's saying. "What did you do to him, Kate?!"

She's yelling. She's yelling at me.

That's when she punches me in the stomach, and I topple right to the ground.

Kate—*Before*

"I feel awful leaving you in this lurch," Stephanie said. Her hands rested on her round belly. "And for being on leave the day of the Tri."

I clucked my tongue. "Stop. It's not like you planned it this way."

Stephanie chuckled. "Definitely not. If my body had listened to all the strategically timed sex Lee and I had, I'd have *had* this baby by now."

She's right. Stephanie had been more than open about her fertility issues. I'd grown accustomed to the Google calendar she shared with me, overrun with data about her period, her ovulation, and five days in a row highlighted in green.

"I wish I was expecting twins," she'd said at one point. "We want two eventually. I had no idea it'd be this hard to get knocked up."

I didn't know what to do but shrug. I've never known quite what to say when people fawn over the twins. It happened a lot while they were babies. People seemed to find it fascinating that there could be two babies who looked almost exactly alike—a boy version and a girl version. Not identical, but unmistakably twins.

And I probably fed into all that by frequently dressing them similarly. Not the same, but similarly. I liked the nice women in the grocery store who smiled approvingly at me. I liked the bank tellers who would give Krista and Keith red suckers, make a joke that both suckers were the same. I liked that I had something people thought was special.

The twins were nearly grown-up now. They just went through driver's training this summer. It's been so long since I've thought of the twins as babies. Lately they've just felt like liabilities—large, hormonal bodies that, at any moment, could crash my car or get drunk at a party, call us from jail. So far, they've been well-behaved kids, but even good kids get rebellious.

But I just smiled and told Stephanie we should get back to business.

We only had two weeks before she was due, and a lot to get through. Even though I'd been her right hand for five years in the Parks and Recreation Department, I'd never hosted the annual Charles E. Belknap Legacy Triathlon—the Belknap Tri. It was Stephanie's baby. It had been hers for the past twenty years. It is far and away the most popular event our department hosts. Hundreds of people sign up for it. Many travel from other states to participate. Proceeds from the event support the Historical Society—a good cause. Local media always cover the event. It's a fun day for spectators, since Reeds Lake is so beautiful. It's too soon to know what the forecast will be, but early September in West

Michigan is usually generous, weather-wise. Last year it was a perfect sixty-four degrees.

Stephanie makes the triathlon an incredible event. She's done well to promote it on social media.

But Stephanie left me in charge of the triathlon while on maternity leave, with Chelsea and Luke, the intern, as extra support. It was up to me to make it great. I told Stephanie over and over it was cool. That I was up for it.

She didn't need to worry, I told her. Everything was under control.

I would have no problem with it at all.

"Come on," I'd told Stephanie. "You can trust me."

Kate—*After*

It takes a moment to figure out why I'm not breathing. It's the hangover; it's making me feel like I'm moving through molasses. That and the fact that I got the wind knocked out of me. I'm still on the ground. I'm aware of how many people saw me fall.

Chelsea is holding my arm again, asking me if I'm okay. The ground is hard under my ass. I wonder if I'll get a bruise. I should be lucky nothing seems broken. Chelsea's lower lip quivers. Despite my discombobulation, I put the pieces together.

Who knew such a small woman could be so strong?

It must be the pregnancy. The woman who punched me is very, very pregnant.

And I know who she is.

It's Madalynn Price. Under her pink and white checked sundress is a bump the size of a basketball. She's beautiful. She's so tiny—the opposite of my build. She must be barely five feet tall. She has long blonde hair. She looks like a child—sort of. I know she's thirty-something. I bet she's a hundred pounds soaking wet—when not pregnant. I might weigh two of her.

I know from stalking her Facebook with Robin, my best friend, that Madalynn and Bryan are expecting their first baby this November.

Were expecting.

He's dead, isn't he? Is he dead?

He looked dead when I saw his body come out of the water. Not that I know what a dead person looks like.

But she's here, and she's pregnant, and I'm not altogether sure she won't punch me again.

"Madalynn," I eke out. I don't know what I want to say, but I want to say something.

My mind flashes back to those pictures I saw of her and Bryan on Facebook.

A maternity photoshoot, Robin had chuckled. I remember that I couldn't believe the man in those pictures was my Bryan. He was posing with her, his hands on her belly, which looked like a snow globe under her gauzy dress. He looked the same, although he was older, of course. So was I. There were wrinkles around his eyes. That's how I looked too, though. We were in our mid-fifties now. I'll be fifty-four this December. He has nearly a year on me. *Had*. He looked happy in all those photos. *Imagine*, Robin had said, *becoming a dad at fifty-five! He'll be seventy-three when the kid finishes high school! Seventy-seven when that kid finishes college!*

Madalynn's hands are balled into fists, but her eyes are on the crowd around her husband. She's staring, too, and like me, she seems unable to move.

He's in the back of the ambulance now, on a stretcher. The paramedics are asking everyone crowded around the edge of the lake to move out of the way of the ambulance. There's an officer here now, too—a tall man with a brown mustache. He's talking to a paramedic—the cute one. I remember I'm in charge. I remember I'm supposed to know what to say. I know it's only a matter of time before I'm asked questions.

I look back at Madalynn. I meet her eye. "I didn't do anything to him."

But she isn't listening. She isn't moving. She's frozen, staring at Bryan's body.

It's like she's drowning, too.

* * *

A knock on the door pulls me from a dream. At least I think I'm dreaming. Everything feels like a blur. The morning's events come back to me as I lay there, blinking, in my own bed.

The racers coming in, confused. People crying. We couldn't stop the rest of the racers, so most of them finished the Tri; they were oblivious until they reached the finish line. Bill didn't read the winners' times. There was no awards presentation. There were no photographs of racers taken on the podium beneath the banner. Bill just handed out medals and trophies. Racers accepted them almost sheepishly, with guilt. A man had died. What did a medal matter?

As far as I could tell, after it happened, people mostly retreated—back to their cars, their homes. Everyone was on their phones. Talking. Texting. Word spread fast.

Paul picked me up. The kids were at friends' houses. Paul talked to me about what happened. He made me tea, then poured me a whiskey, then ordered me into my pajamas and into our bed.

Paul's face appears in the crack of the bedroom door separating from its frame. I try to sit up when Stephanie's face appears behind Paul. It takes me a moment to put two and two together—to put my supervisor in this new context.

Stephanie has been to my house before, but not my bedroom.

"Hi," I say. Thanks to the nap, the gnawing headache has mostly disappeared. I smooth the cream-colored comforter covering my lap. I hope she doesn't notice the clothes piled on the chair.

"I'm sorry to wake you," she says. She's wearing dark gray yoga pants and a blue loose-fitting wrap over a white t-shirt. She's carrying a car seat.

Liliana. Her new daughter. She must be sleeping. I haven't even had time to bring her a meal. I'd planned to bake lasagna.

From the door, Paul shoots me a look that asks if I need anything. His fingers are still on the door's edge. I'm touched by how protective of me he feels since it happened.

Stephanie sits on the edge of the bed and sets the car seat at her feet. Liliana is sleeping.

"What time is it?"

"Just after four."

"Whoa. I can't believe Paul let me nap that long."

"He's worried about you. I am too."

She reaches over and squeezes my hand.

"I want to see your baby!" I can't believe I'm meeting her baby this way. It feels so wrong. "I'm sorry, I'm all out of sorts. How are things? How is she? Are you sleeping? How's breast-feeding?"

Stephanie sighs and smiles as she looks at Liliana. "It's okay. I'm exhausted. Lee is a big help. But I want to hear about you. What happened?"

I draw in a big breath. "I still don't know. I mean, everything was going fine. We got the cones up yesterday, as you know, the signs—temporary orders not to park on the street. Chelsea handled packet pickup—that went fine. Luke was running around answering last minute questions. I got there around 5:30. The racers started to arrive shortly after that. I marked the transition areas…"

I realize I'm describing an event Stephanie knows so well she could run it in her sleep. But the process of recounting the morning step by step is helping me focus. I continue.

"We started right on time. The divers were in the water. We had the boats out—volunteers in place. Photographers in place. Water station, first aid station—everything set up. We got the swimmers organized by age group, you know, and they went into the water, in heats. We had waves going in every three minutes, just to help them spread out a little… and then…"

"Then what?"

"Then…" I trail off.

"Kate?"

"Yeah?"

"What happened *then*?"

"Then Chelsea grabbed me by the arm and started to pull me down to the water. She said something had happened. She said someone had drowned. The rest, I don't know..."

"Kate." Stephanie shakes her head. I'm not sure how to take her tone.

"It was an accident."

"Yes," Stephanie says. "I know that."

"Everybody signs the liability waiver."

Stephanie looks at me then. I don't understand the look on her face.

I press on. "We aren't responsible. We can't be. He would have signed the form saying he was in good enough health to undertake the Tri. It would have been his responsibility to get proper medical clearance, and, to be honest with you, I'm not sure he was in that great of shape. At least he didn't look—"

Stephanie puts her hand up. From her feet come a few stirring cries. I've been too loud.

"I know all that," Stephanie says softly.

"Of course you do," I rush. "You can quote the waiver better than I can."

Stephanie is crouching by the foot of the bed, rocking the car seat. She seems to be coaxing the baby into not needing a feeding right at this moment.

"Kate," Stephanie says quietly. Once again, I don't know how to read her tone. "A man died today. We need to talk about your role in it."

Kate—*Before*

I was sitting at Stephanie's desk when Chelsea came in for our meeting, decked out in her usual outfit: pencil skirt, colorful blouse, cardigan to keep her warm in the chilly building. She always looked so professional, so put-together. I knew I could take some tips from her; my outfits were often wrinkled—garments I grabbed from the wingback chair in our bedroom and decided, *this'll do.*

There were many perks of being Stephanie's stand-in: her parking spot, for one. It was also nice having an office with a door I could close.

But above everything, I couldn't get used to this view. God bless whoever thought to locate the Parks and Recreation Department in a building so close to Reeds Lake. A pair of sailboats moved gracefully, sleek as doves, right outside my window.

I cleared my throat.

The perks had not worn off, but one thing was for sure: I was not used to being the Interim Director. I was not used to overseeing Chelsea, or Luke for that matter. I wasn't used to being someone else's supervisor. I wasn't sure I liked it.

"I printed this out," Chelsea chuckled. "I don't know why. We really don't need a hard copy. Plus, there are still, like, ten days left, so we may get some additions. Or cancelations."

I smiled. Right away, I gleaned what this printed list was: a list of the triathletes who paid eighty-five dollars to compete in this year's event.

I could see fields for name, age, gender, city, t-shirt size, emergency contact, and a phone number for said emergency contact. Another field affirmed that the participant had signed the liability waver. Another gave race organizers permission to take and use photographs on social media and for promotional activities.

Then I saw a name. It popped up at me from page twelve of Chelsea's printout.

I'd know that name anywhere.

"What?" Chelsea asked. I must have gasped or made some other kind of audible sound.

"Nothing." Then I snickered.

"We *do* have a lot of older registrants," Chelsea said. Then, a worried look crossed her face. "Not that fifty-something is old! I don't mean that. I just mean that this event always seems to attract, you know, older adults, too. Which is great!"

Which made me grin. Chelsea couldn't be more than thirty. Recently married. I wasn't certain she wanted kids. If *they* wanted kids.

She never gave any hint. She'd blanked on what to write on the card I got for Stephanie's baby shower.

"It's not that." I hesitated. She thought she'd insulted me. I felt compelled to assure her she hadn't.

I pointed at the paper. The line read: *Bryan Price, Male, Rockford, Size L, Madalynn Price.*

"I know that guy."

"Oh," Chelsea said. "Cool."

But I'd said it in a way that indicated it might not have been cool.

"See that little asterisk by his name?" she asked.

I nodded.

"That means this is his first time doing the Belknap Tri."

"Ah."

We both examined the page for a long moment. When I looked up, I saw Chelsea staring at me with a curious look.

I grinned and decided to give in. "We were married."

"Oh!" Chelsea said, her shock sincere. "I had no idea!"

"Why would you? It was forever ago. I knew he lived near here, but I didn't know he was so close."

Chelsea scrunched her nose. She was loving this, I could tell. This disclosure was giving us a chance to bond. "You hate him, huh?"

"No. I don't."

"Not even a little?" She was smiling again.

I sat back in my chair, my eyes flitting to the window, to the shimmering waters of Reeds Lake. In the late afternoon, the sunlight shattered on the water like diamonds.

"I don't think about him," I said. "It feels like another life. Gosh… I mean, it was twenty years ago. Something like that. How much everything has changed since then—when I was young and dumb. Now I'm just old and dumb."

Chelsea was waiting for me to continue and not being shy about it, making it clear that she would take however much of this story I wanted to tell.

"I don't mean to put you on the spot," Chelsea said. "I mean, I do, but I don't."

I smiled and shook my head. I'd woken up too late to have time to do anything to my hair. I'd just thrown it in a bun and hoped for the best. I'd been wearing my hair that way almost exclusively since Stephanie had handed me the reins.

It might be my imagination, but I swore Chelsea was leaning forward, like she was hanging on my every word.

"I don't mind talking about it—I really don't. It's just that there isn't much to tell. We were high school sweethearts. We went to different colleges. We broke up that first semester. See, I'm putting myself to sleep! This is more boring than the end-of-month expense reports. Which—by the way—due soon."

Chelsea laughed. "Well, I don't really feel like going back to my desk yet. And I certainly don't feel like scanning receipts."

I sighed. "We dated other people, you know, me and Bryan. But we kept in touch. We got back together senior year. By that time, I had transferred, and to be honest, I hadn't met anyone. I guess he was just always in the back of my mind. A few months before graduation, he suggested we go on Spring Break together—"

"Now we're getting somewhere!"

I chuckled again. I remembered the way he was on that vacation: that trip to the Keys. It had felt so far from home. I'd never been to Florida, and from the minute he'd asked, I had been flooded with excitement. I had pictures of that trip still—in a box somewhere. Not with the rest of my photos, but still. I'd kept them. Those photos were why I had such clear images of how Bryan was on that trip—the Spring Break we decided to really give us a go. Bryan in a ball cap, that gray t-shirt he always wore. The cheap fast-food. My pink bikini.

"Bryan proposed on that trip," I continued. Chelsea's eyes were wide. "It was sweet. He snuck away at a gift shop, bought me this turquoise ring. I mean, we got a real one later. We married that fall—at the courthouse. I didn't want a big wedding anyway. A few friends came, and our parents, of course. No bridal party, though. I *did* wear a white dress—one I found at Macy's. More like cream, but it was cute. I don't know what else to tell. We moved to our first apartment, just east of—gosh, near 28th Street. One bedroom. Man, was that place tiny. Everything was okay for, I don't know, the first few months."

"Then what happened?"

I hesitated.

"Come on," she urged. "You've taken me this far. Why did you two break up?"

I noticed she'd used the kinder word. Break up—not divorce. I hadn't thought about this in so long, I felt my voice catch in my throat for just a moment. I blinked.

"It fell apart. I moved in with a friend—at first just to get space. But things didn't get better. Then… Well, he gave me an ultimatum. I remember that. I had to do what he said, or it was over." I was avoiding the d-word, too.

Chelsea's eyes widened again. "That's dumb. I mean, when do ultimatums ever work?"

"That sounds like a question Carrie Bradshaw would ask."

Chelsea grinned. I'm relieved she caught my *Sex and the City* reference.

I'm also relieved she didn't ask what the ultimatum was.

* * *

I wondered about giving Paul the play-by-play of my conversation with Chelsea that day—how we'd found Bryan's name on the list of registrants, clocked the asterisk by his name that meant this was his first Belknap Tri.

Somehow, the man who had never been into cardio while we were married was suddenly running a triathlon. The man who had always carried twenty extra pounds on his frame—even when we were in our twenties—was suddenly an endurance athlete.

But I supposed that wasn't fair of me. We were young when we were together.

People change—of course they do! Bryan Price had changed because we all change. Why would I expect him to be trapped in amber? I certainly wasn't.

Typically, over dinner, Paul and I talked about our days. The kids, too—if they were home. Keith had soccer practice in the spring, Krista had a hundred friends to attend to with crises all their own: breakups, first dates, midterms.

I thought perhaps I wouldn't talk about Bryan in front of the kids. But I would tell Paul. We weren't big on secrets. This wouldn't be something I would keep from him. I could picture pouring us each a glass of red wine and watching his face as I recounted the story.

"You'll never guess who came up at work today," I could say.

"Who?" Paul would ask.

And I would tell him how it was Bryan, and how strange it was to think about the events of two decades ago.

Paul would ask something to extent of, *will it be weird to see him?* And I would give my sweet husband the same answer I gave Chelsea: not weird. Just a little like *déjà vu*. It might feel like watching an old movie on TV and fighting the niggling feeling that I've seen this one before.

I was already preparing myself to see Bryan again, after so much time. I assumed I'd see him on race day in just over a week.

I was readying myself to compare the two Bryans: the one of now

(*55, Male, Rockford, Size L, Madalynn Price*) to the one I married (*25, Male, Grand Rapids, Size XL, Kate Turner*).

The Bryan I married at the courthouse kept his cash wadded in his back pocket. He forgot his mother's birthday. Most of his underwear had holes. He was constantly worried about money. That first year, we were cash poor. That was why we'd married at the courthouse. There wasn't enough to do anything else. He kept careful track of his paychecks and mine, all our monthly expenses, including the student loans that came due fast.

I used to think maybe that stress broke us. It's like we jumped headfirst into the ocean together. No gradual wading into adulthood. Suddenly, we tried to be each other's everything. We never built a solid foundation. We barely knew one another.

With Paul, it was the other way. I got to know Paul gradually. We were friends first. He knew I was divorced and that I wanted to take things slow. I trusted him before I ever kissed him. When he proposed after two years, the yes was an easy one.

But I knew it wasn't the stress that had broken Bryan and me apart.

Nor was it the money. Nor the fighting. It wasn't that we weren't friends, or that we weren't close enough. It wasn't that he had cheated or I had cheated.

No.

Something far darker had made me run.

Madalynn—*After*

Yes, I know about Kate Barkway.

And yes—she deserved that punch.

It's her fault this happened. Bryan spent months using a snorkel to aid his breathing while he swam, and maybe she didn't know that, but she should have let him keep it. Obviously he'd trained with it, if he didn't tell her; it's not like he randomly brought it on race day—do you know what I mean? She's so stupid and her mistake—her *decision*—cost me everything.

Us everything.

I knew she was stupid from the stories Bryan used to tell about her, though to be honest, he didn't talk about her often. She wasn't important. She only came up a handful of times. She was a *mistake*. Marrying her was a mistake and thank God he'd gotten out of it.

They hadn't been married long. They split, he went back to school—graduate school—and everything from then on was fine—all steps in the long road that led to marrying me.

Of course I Googled her, as I had searched for all his ex-girlfriends. She wasn't even the ex he talked about the most! Bryan dated a woman named Felicia for a year and a half—a gorgeous, red-headed therapist. Honestly, Felicia was the one who made my heckles go up.

Kate Barkway? Please.

Kate Barkway is an overweight, menopausal wench with kids in their teens. I felt zero threatened by her.

But yes, he'd told me about his brief first marriage. What couple doesn't go over their dating history? Although, parsing out that information is an art. I'd practiced it a few times before getting to Bryan, and I was sure he'd practiced it a few times before he started dating me.

I had one serious relationship in high school. No sex. Too young.

Three semi-serious relationships in college. Sex. Lots of sex.

One serious relationship after college. That was my longest one, but it ended maturely. Ken. He moved for his job, and I didn't want to go. We tried long distance for two months, but in the end, it was a good reason to go our separate ways. I talked to him for weeks on the phone as he settled into his new apartment. I made one trip to California, and that was enough for us to say it was time to move on.

Then I met Bryan Price.

People always say love finds you when you aren't looking for it. This is true.

I met Bryan at the airport on my return flight from San

Francisco, right after Ken and I broke up. I'm not making this up. Bryan and I met at baggage claim—how perfect is that? It was taking so long, and I was mad at myself for checking luggage. I should have crammed everything into my carry-on, but Ken had planned hiking excursions and fancy dinners out, and I had wanted to look good.

It was late on a Sunday night. I took a break from scanning the carousel to notice the cute guy standing a few feet away. Honestly, all I wanted to do was go home take a hot shower and go to bed. My eyes were puffy. I was emotionally drained, felt like shit from all the crying, and the time change was making it even harder to stay focused.

I wasn't in the mood to talk, but I clocked Bryan studying me out of the corner of my eye. When he eventually said *hi*, I wanted to shut him down at first. Twenty-four hours ago, I was sitting on Ken's kitchen floor, crying. We'd just decided to end our relationship. The last thing I wanted was a new man.

But there was a part of me that had been curious about Bryan, so I smiled back. He seemed so much older, so much more mature. I was already wondering what it might be like to date someone older—someone more established in his career. Someone clearer on what he wanted out of life. What he wanted in a woman. He made some comment about how our luggage should get frequent flyer miles, too. It didn't make sense, but I'd laughed anyway.

"You live in Grand Rapids?" he'd asked.

I'd nodded carefully. Best not to give too much information to strange men. But he immediately told me he did, too, and where he worked, and that he had spent the week in California on a business trip.

That's when I realized we had been on the *same flight.*

Whenever people asked how we met, sometimes I liked to tell them we met on an airplane, and sometimes I liked to tell them we met at baggage claim.

I wasn't sure which story was more romantic.

The first gave people the image that maybe we were seated next to each other and started talking, and then three hours later, we'd told each other our life stories and had fallen in love.

I liked that story, even though it never happened.

With the latter, it was more of a meet-cute: two people at baggage claim waiting for their suitcases to join them. They strike up a flirtation, and then the next thing you know, he's asking for her number. Baggage claim. What a perfect way to describe the way I was that night. Yet despite all that, there was Bryan Price, chatting with me for a good ten minutes and making sure that before he walked away with his suitcase on wheels, he had asked for my number.

I know it's cliché to say everything was perfect after that and we lived happily ever after.

But everything was fucking perfect after that night, and up until the day Kate Barkway murdered my husband, we were living happily ever after.

Kate—*After*

All eyes are on me as I walk through the door. Normally, I might stop and chat with Cecilia at reception, but not today.

Today, I make a beeline to Stephanie Hoover's office—my office—plodding quickly on the carpet, avoiding eye contact with everyone.

Chelsea's text had prompted me to shower, throw on some clothes, get to the office as soon as possible. *An officer is here and wants to talk to you, when are you coming in??*

My heart is beating hard in my chest. The door to Stephanie's office is open. Chelsea's sitting at the small conference table across from an officer in uniform—a handsome, middle-aged man with very little hair. His arms are crossed. On the table, his notepad lays open. I'm glad to see Chelsea has served him coffee.

He turns his attention to me as I approach the table. I'm struck by his blue eyes—a bright shade. Pretty. He stands to shake my hand.

"Ted Dorsey," he says. He gestures at the empty chair next to Chelsea. "Would you join us?"

I nod. I know I'm not in trouble. There's no way I'm in trouble.

In fact, Chelsea's text was a bit of a misdirection.

Officer Dorsey isn't exactly a police officer. East Grand Rapids combined its police and fire department, which together comprise Public Safety. But the cops were unarmed.

And I'm pretty sure I've run into Ted Dorsey before. His building is next door. How many times over the years have we exchanged polite smiles as we parked our cars near one another, bumped into each other at the vending machines? Now that I'm sitting across from him, I'm certain we've met.

But it doesn't seem like the time to tell him.

"Would you like me to stay?" Chelsea asks.

"No, that's okay."

Then I realize Chelsea was asking Officer Dorsey—not me. My face reddens.

Why am I still out of it? I telepathically ask Chelsea for coffee, too. I've only had one cup while getting ready, and I need more of a jolt to get through this day.

"I appreciate your help, Ms. Schmidt. I think I'll be all set with Ms. Barkway."

Chelsea leaves with an awkward half-smile.

"Though to be honest with you, there's not much to discuss," he says as soon as she's closed the door behind her.

My heart rate slows a little with the news. "I'll help any way I can."

"Appreciate that," he says, looking at his notebook. There are a few dozen lines written down—half sentences, a few words circled. I can't really read his handwriting. "We follow up on every death that occurs within city limits. We did have an officer arrive at the scene of the triathlon yesterday morn—"

"That's right," I say. Then feel sheepish for interrupting. "I mean, I remember. Officer Thorpe."

Officer Dorsey nods. If he's annoyed, he's not letting it show. His face is chiseled from marble.

Calm down, I tell myself. I force a deep breath.

I feel nervous for no reason. I have nothing to hide.

"We're currently awaiting the results of the autopsy. That should be done within the week. I'm basically here, Ms. Barkway, to talk to you, as I understand you are the Director—"

"*Interim* Director."

God, I really should stop interrupting an officer of the law, even if he is just from Public Safety. I have very little experience being in trouble. Certainly, I've never been questioned by authorities. Not even the school principal.

I need to relax.

I'm acting like I'm guilty.

"That's right. Stephanie Hoover's the Director of Parks. I know Stephanie. She auctioned off a weekend at her place on Crystal Lake for the Spring fundraiser."

"She's on maternity leave," I offer. "She just had her baby. I mean, literally—like the other day. A girl. She's beautiful. And Stephanie's doing fine."

Shut up, I say to myself.

Is it possible I am still hungover? I'd read about hangovers lasting more than one day. It was also possible I was dehydrated. I'd barely had anything to eat or drink since it happened. Just the food Paul forced in front of me. He'd suggested I stay home from work today, and I had planned to until Chelsea texted.

Officer Dorsey meets my eye. "What can you tell me about what happened yesterday? Any sense of perspective you can give will be helpful."

I pause a long moment, then recount everything the way I had to Stephanie in my bedroom: what time I arrived, what Luke and Chelsea were doing, how everything had been going according to plan. The event had been running like clockwork.

"The swimmers entered the lake at the designated place," I say. "And—I don't know—only five minutes went by, or so, maybe six or seven. And then there was panic at the water."

"You were still at the registration table when Mr. Price was in the water?"

"I was. I was tidying up and getting ready to walk down, just to see if—well, I don't know *what*, really. I've never run a race before." I laugh at my pun. "I mean, literally. I've never run a race before. I mean, look at me—I'm not exactly in shape."

Officer Dorsey doesn't laugh at the joke I make at my own expense.

"I mean in the sense of, I've never overseen a race before. The Belknap is Stephanie's, for sure. I wasn't certain where to be, if that makes sense. But the event typically runs so smoothly, I didn't think I would have anything to do other than smile and say congratulations. Give them their trophies and prize money, you know?"

Officer Dorsey frowns. He looks back at his notebook and, with a stray hand, flips back a page. Then he sets the notebook down and folds his hands over his lean stomach.

Go on, his eyes seem to say.

"Then I—you know, there was the commotion and the siren. The ambulance got there. Chelsea let me know that a swimmer's body was pulled out of the water and… it was awful."

I close my eyes. I can't believe that was yesterday. This has been the longest twenty-four hours of my life, and that's saying a lot. With the twins, when they were young, there were so many endless days—so many tedious hours of exhaustion and monotony. I thought those days of feeling like butter spread over too much bread were over for me.

"I'm sure it was," he says. His voice softens. "So, you were not near the water when Mr. Price drowned?"

I shake my head. "No. Honestly, I was so tired. I had woken up so early, you know? I just—it took me a long time to understand what happened. They put—the medics put him in the ambulance. One person did CPR. Chelsea said he wasn't breathing. But I don't think she—she must have just heard someone else say that? I didn't know if he was dead."

Officer Dorsey nods his head lightly, thinking. He's a good listener. Surreptitiously, I glance at the clock on the wall. It's just after ten. Hopefully when this interview is over, I can get that second cup of coffee and something to eat.

Better yet, go home. Crawl under the covers. Welcome the

darkness.

"We had a complaint from Madalynn Price—the wife. She says you and Bryan used to be married."

I nod. I should have mentioned that. It would have been normal to mention my connection to Bryan.

Now it looks like I'm trying to hide it.

Officer Dorsey had asked me to recount the events of the day. My marriage to Bryan… that was from a different lifetime.

"I figured you knew that already," I chuckle.

He doesn't smile. "When was this?"

"Oh gosh," I chuckle again. I rub my palms on my thighs. The waistband of my pants digs into my belly. "1990 through early '91. Not long at all, really. Barely had time to write the thank you cards."

He nods but again doesn't laugh at my joke. He writes the dates down in his notebook. I wonder if I should add that technically it wasn't until early 1992 that the divorce was official. I don't, though.

He continues, "Madalynn Price also indicated you changed a rule?"

I freeze.

Maybe I am still hungover. I am still not putting thoughts together.

"Not specifically, no," I answer. "I didn't change a rule."

Officer Dorsey looks at me.

I continue. "There was a question at the beginning of the event about gear—a snorkel for the swimming portion."

He looks at me again like, *go on*.

"When asked, I made the choice to disallow snorkels. I thought—well, according to the rules, swimmers aren't supposed to have equipment that could give them an advantage."

Officer Dorsey frowns. I hope I'm as convincing as a lawyer.

"Swimmers can have goggles, but they can't have, you know, flippers or anything like that. Nothing that can propel them."

"You thought snorkels fell under that category of equipment that could *propel*?"

I nod.

Then I shake my head.

That's not exactly right, is it?

I'm not sure what else to tell Officer Dorsey. Should I tell him my judgment was bad because I was hungover? Because I had never overseen the race before? That I didn't know the answer? That I was tired of everyone looking to me for answers? Never wanted to be Interim

Director in the first place?

"I didn't—unfortunately, I didn't have access to that information. If snorkels specifically are allowed. And I didn't have a fast way to contact Stephanie. My understanding had been that no additional gear beyond goggles was permitted for the swimmers. That's what I enforced."

"And you later learned that they *should* have been allowed?"

I freeze again. I force my breathing to slow. "I suppose. I mean, in hindsight, I should have just said *sure*. But I thought, you know, like I said, I thought the fair thing was to say no additional stuff. I just wanted to keep it fair, you know? The cash prize is big, and I wanted it to be fair who wins it. Plus, that's the thing about hindsight: it's always twenty-twenty."

I wonder if he's thinking what I'm not voicing: if I'd let Bryan have that fucking snorkel, he'd still be alive today.

Officer Dorsey writes something else down in his notepad. I wonder if I've said too much. I said the word "fair" a bunch of times. And quoted that dumb cliché about hindsight.

But it's not like the rules only applied to one person. A rule applies to everyone. Officer Dorsey would know that. I wasn't being unfair. I was interpreting the guidance as best I could to the best of my ability, given the circumstances.

I wonder if I should say all that, or if it would make me look defensive.

I wonder when this is going to be over.

He said Madalynn had a complaint. About me. I wonder if that means she's filed charges.

"She punched me, you know," I say, as his pen is still on his paper. "She tell you that?"

He looks up from his pad and frowns. "Who?"

"Madalynn Price."

"She *punched* you?" He says the word punched carefully. His face says he doesn't believe me. It does feel like a stretch. I'm much bigger than her, pregnancy aside. She had shock and anger on her side, though, and I had only had my hangover.

I nod. "I fell. Bruised my tailbone." I hope this last detail garners some sympathy.

He frowns harder, cocks his head. "Was Officer Thorpe present at that time?"

I shake my head.

"Any witnesses?"

I nod. "There was a crowd. Of course, they were more concerned about… you know."

"When exactly, yesterday, did this punch occur?"

"When she saw me. Right after they pulled Bryan's body out."

He's staring. He's good at not giving away what he concludes, but he makes it easy to tell that he's weighing the words.

"And you didn't press charges against Ms. Price?"

I shake my head. "No. I think Madalynn was in shock, you know? And she—she was angry. And she, you know, like any new wife, I suppose she…" I let my voice trail off.

"She what?"

"Well, I suppose she doesn't like me much."

At least we're no longer talking about the snorkel, I think.

"Would you describe your relationship with Madalynn as fraught?"

"I would describe it as non-existent. I'd never spoken to her before yesterday, and I hadn't spoken to Bryan for… gosh, probably for two decades? I don't even know. We were not a part of one another's lives. I think Madalynn was aware of me from, you know, whatever Bryan chose to share." A pause. "Plus, with social media, I think she probably had that general awareness of who I am. You know how those things go."

"What things?"

I shrug. I think if he were a woman, I wouldn't have to explain this. "People Google their partner's exes, you know. Just… it's something to do. I don't know."

He smiles a little now. I clock a gold wedding band on his finger. It's probably been a number of years since he's given any thought to his wife's exes.

"Wait," I say, "are you saying Madalynn is pressing charges against me?"

Now the frown on his face is deeper than ever. "No. On what grounds would she? She's the one who punched you, right?"

I shrug. His words reverberate in my head. I don't say, she thinks I murdered her husband. I say, "I don't know, I'm just—sorry. You said she complained."

My eyes well up with tears. It seems to soften Officer Dorsey.

"Look. You've been through a lot—both you and Ms. Price. Once we get the autopsy, we'll complete the report. Multiple witnesses attested the victim was overwhelmed in the water. It's also possible he had a heart issue or experienced an aneurysm—that's what the coroner's report will tell us. As for Ms. Price—"

"I'm sure she was just overwhelmed," I repeat. Why was

interrupting an officer a new disease of mine? "She was in shock. And you know she's very pregnant."

A small smile appears on his face. He looks like he might laugh, but he doesn't.

"You have kids?" I ask.

He nods. "Four. All boys."

He looks wistful for a moment, then turns back to his notepad.

After a quick glance, he closes it, then straightens in his chair. "Well, Ms. Barkway, I think that's it." He stands. "I'm sorry this happened on your watch. It's a great event. I've had friends do it. Never in twenty years has something like this happened."

I nod. The 21st Charles E. Belknap Legacy Triathlon is the last thing on my mind.

Officer Dorsey reaches into his pocket and produces a business card.

I laugh. "I know where to find you. You're literally next door."

He smiles. "Force of habit."

I walk him to the door.

"If you think of anything else," he says, "feel free to let me know. Sometimes added information brings comfort to the relatives of the deceased."

At that, I pause. I'm aware that Chelsea is watching us from her desk.

"I think this was Bryan's first triathlon," I add. "He wasn't terribly athletic when we were married. Of course, that was a lifetime ago."

Officer Dorsey meets my eyes, but he doesn't take his notebook out. He tells me to have a good rest of my day, and that he hopes I can go home and get some rest.

What I don't add: Bryan Price used to hate the water—especially deep water. He used to avoid swimming at all costs.

I don't tell Officer Dorsey that Bryan Price was very, very afraid of water.

* * *

At lunch, I say nothing to Chelsea as I walk out of the Parks and Recs office. I head to the vending area in the basement. I feed a few dollar bills to the machine and consider my options.

This is the reason my shorts were tight this past summer. But right now, I'm allowing myself to have whatever combination of salt and sugar and fat I want. A Snicker's bar. A bag of trail mix with M&Ms. A can of real Coke.

I toss the items into my bag and continue down the hallway to the double doors leading to the pavilion. There's a picnic table and a handful of wooden benches—an area well maintained with rubber mulch and colorful hydrangeas. From any of the seats, the view of Reeds Lake is perfect. There aren't many people around this morning, which is nice.

The Coke opens with a satisfying hiss. I take a bite of the Snickers and gaze at the lake.

No one would ever know there was a triathlon here Sunday. Yesterday. God. The banner's gone—the one that listed local and corporate sponsors. There are few signs there were hundreds of athletes and onlookers. I do see a recycling bin overflowing with empty bottles, and one errant banana peel on the ground. The maintenance crew will be by later. They are so good about never leaving trash on the grass for long.

There is certainly no indication a man died here.

There's no yellow tape blocking off a crime scene.

Because this *isn't* a crime scene. This is still a small, idyllic, inland lake. The crown jewel of East Grand Rapids. Bad things don't happen here.

With the next bite, I savor the caramel on my tongue. Otherwise, I am numb.

I finish the candy bar and take out my cell. I open the Facebook app.

I blink.

The top post is from my friend Bridget. *This is so tragic*, she wrote. She's linked the news article about Bryan's death. The post has 39 comments. I skim.

He was such a nice guy, one said. *Praying for his family.*

This is just awful, said the next one. *Heartbreaking.*

The next comment tagged Madalynn Price; her name appears in blue. I click it.

There she is. Her profile picture is clearly from that maternity shoot I looked at a few months back with Robin: Bryan standing behind his wife, lovingly caressing Madalynn's stomach. Her face is serene. She looks angelic.

I'm not friends with Madalynn Price, so I can only see parts on her profile: employment, relationship status, education. She has a thousand friends. I can only see part of her wall.

Madalynn, I'm so sorry.

I'm thinking of you and your baby girl.

Madalynn oh my gosh, my heart is breaking for you.

If you need anything at all please call me.

Madalynn I can't fathom your loss.

Please reach out if you need anything.

An outpouring of sympathy. Twenty-four hours ago, she became a widow.

I take another sip of Coke, look at my watch. I should get back. But I can't tear myself away from Madalynn's Facebook.

I click on the option for photographs. I scroll through ten then twenty then thirty of Madalynn. Shot after shot of Madalynn with friends, toasting mimosas, with a group of girlfriends in fedoras. In another she is clearly at a baby shower, moved to tears by a card she's reading. She is stunning. She could be a model.

I feel a stab of jealousy. Clearly Madalynn subsists off a seaweed and kale diet, for a figure like hers. She's adorable pregnant. I only remember wearing oversized house dresses and Paul's old fleeces. Madalynn clearly buys maternity-specific clothing.

I remember it'd seemed like a silly thing to spend money on—clothing only meant to be worn for a few months. But Madalynn is leaning into the pregnancy look.

Have I never done this before? Looked this closely at her? At them? None of these photos look familiar. I click on Bryan's name. I haven't looked at his page in years, maybe. He looks—

Well, I can't escape the thought that he looks *better* now than he did when we were married. Older, sure, but somehow, he just looks brighter. Aside from some thinning hair and the wrinkles, he looks better. He looks *happier*, I realize.

In all the photos on his page, he looks really, really happy.

Golfing with friends. On vacation with Madalynn. I can't tell where they are, but maybe Hawaii? It looks tropical. Bryan with a corgi—the same dog featured on Madalynn's page.

I scroll back. There are no public comments on his wall for four months—not since he'd last changed his profile picture. I frown. Must be for friends only. Or maybe people didn't do that. I mean, how weird would it be to post a comment on someone's page who just died?

Finally, I scroll over to the little blue rectangle that says message and impulsively click it. On my screen is a blank box, a blinking cursor.

I stare down. I could type anything.

When I told Officer Dorsey that I hadn't spoken to Bryan Price in two decades, that was not exactly true.

I happened to spot him about a year ago in a grocery store north of town near the produce section. Krista had been with me. It was a

Friday. Paul was on a fishing weekend with Kevin. I didn't normally shop at this store, but Krista and I had dropped the boys off at the Park and Ride near 10 mile. It had been on the way home, and I'd promised Krista we'd make pizza for dinner.

When I'd spotted Bryan, I'd felt my blood run cold, my pulse race. Immediately, I'd lost the thread of whatever Krista was saying. He spotted me staring at him as our cart approached his, passing him by the cantaloupe.

I'd smiled and said *hi*. He'd smiled back, simply, and said *hello*.

The encounter was over before I could even process it. By the time we picked Paul and Kevin up Sunday night from that same Park and Ride, it'd been completely forgotten.

But Krista, pushing our cart, had asked who that man was I'd greeted.

Just an old friend, I'd said as Krista pushed the cart onward.

The cursor is still blinking. I hold the phone tight.

Nice to see you changed your mind, I write.

I hit send before I can give it another thought.

Kate—*After*

Tuesday, first thing, I head into Conference Room C. It's been forty-eight hours since Bryan Price's body was pulled out of the water.

Stephanie Hoover's here. She's not *back*-back—meaning, she's not back from maternity leave. But she's here today. Lee is at home with the baby; she has a few hours. She called a special meeting of the team. No one will say it, but I know it's damage control.

Chelsea, Marilyn, Trace, and Bill are already gathered. Without meaning to be, I'm the last to arrive. I glance at my watch as I sit in the last available chair between Chelsea and Marilyn. I want to emphasize to them that I'm only, like, one minute behind.

"Hi, Kate," Stephanie says.

"Hi, everyone," I say, scooting up to the table. It's clear that Stephanie is in charge—of the room, of our team. Her energy reminds everyone of that fact. I realize I'm relieved Stephanie's here. I can relax. I can remove the word *interim* from my vocabulary for an hour.

"I won't keep you long," Stephanie begins. It's not the usual *how was your weekend* or *what's new with you* icebreaker. "I told Lee I'd be home by noon. That's around the next feeding." She pauses to smile. She must be so tired. She's still so polished. She looks nice in her blue sweater dress. Her stomach still shows the telltale pouch, but she looks amazing.

"I just want to check in with you all after what happened Sunday."

Everyone looks grim. I study the patch of table in front of me.

"It's hard to know where to begin," Stephanie says. "Of course, nothing like this has ever happened in the history of the event. I wish I'd been there. But from what I've heard, you *all* did an incredible job in the, uh, aftermath. Helping first responders, informing the athletes, and corralling people together. Amazing. So, I want to thank you for that."

But all I hear is Stephanie saying, *I gave the event to Kate one fucking time. Look how she screwed up. Look at the mess she made.*

Around the table there are small nods. "And Luke," Chelsea adds. He's not in this meeting, and I'm glad.

Stephanie nods enthusiastically. "Yes. absolutely. Luke, too. He was so helpful. I called him Sunday night."

"Is he okay?" Marilyn asks.

"Yes," Stephanie says. "I think so. He was shaken up, but I know you all were. Especially you, Kate," she says. She looks at me.

Then I feel everyone's eyes on me. I nod. They all must be aware by now that I'm the victim's ex-wife, though I only ever told Chelsea. "Yes." It's like everyone is waiting for me to continue, but I don't, so the eyes drift back to the woman who commands the room.

"I've been contacted by MLive for comment. If any of you are—as I stated in my email Sunday—you can direct them to me. That's perfectly acceptable."

"We're not canceling the event going forward, are we?" Marilyn asks.

Stephanie shakes her head. "No. No I don't think so. I don't think we should. I don't think that'd be the right thing to do. Although I am thinking about..." she pauses. "I've been thinking about what we could do for the family. His wife, who I understand is pregnant. We may want to donate all proceeds to his family, for instance. These are just ideas, and I welcome your suggestions."

"We should take up a collection among us," Marilyn says. "Parks and Recs."

"That's a fantastic idea," Stephanie says. "Would you—would you put that together? Maybe see if we can make it a community thing?"

"I think there's already a GoFundMe," Chelsea pipes in. "But I can help you with that, if you would like, Marilyn."

"Oh please do. You know I'm bad with Internet stuff."

There is a collective good-natured smile—Marilyn hates the Internet—then the tense feeling of the room returns. The heaviness of what happened returns.

We all saw a dead body. That's called a corpse.

Well, he was mostly dead when he was pulled from the water. He was alive, but he may as well have been dead. Bryan Price never woke up at the hospital, according to Officer Dorsey. He never said final words.

I wonder what it feels like to drown.

"Is there anything else..." Stephanie says. "We've processed all the requests for reimbursement so far, right?"

Chelsea nods. "Yes. I did set the deadline as you suggested for the end of the month, you know, to give people time, but so far, only about a dozen people have requested their money back. I think most people are okay with deferring to next year—pushing that registration payment forward or, like, just not worrying about it and letting it be a donation. I like that idea that we'll give the money to his family."

Stephanie nods. The fact that hundreds of disappointed athletes who trained for months went home without completing their races seems to be the last thing on anyone's mind.

"Okay," Stephanie says. She has both palms on the table. "I also just want to remind everyone that our health insurance covers up to five counseling sessions with a trained counselor every year at no cost. That's a covered benefit through EAP. It's confidential, so please visit the website or call the number for an appointment if you feel like you need to talk to someone."

More nods.

She's so much better at this than I am.

I wonder if she regrets naming me Interim Director. Of course she is. *What a mistake*, she's thinking. She should have picked Chelsea. Even Internet-hating Marilyn would have done a better job than me.

"Are you all feeling…" she starts. "I don't mean to put anyone on the spot. Are you all okay? I know this has been difficult. This was one of those things—not something anyone could have predicted." I can't help but notice she's stopped short of using the phrase *it wasn't anyone here's fault.*

I also can't help but notice she isn't saying anything about the conversation we had in my bedroom. She isn't bringing up the elephant in the room: he asked for a snorkel, and I said no.

"Are there any questions?"

"Has the coroner's report come back?" It's Bill.

"Not yet," Stephanie says. "Or if it has, Officer Dorsey hasn't let me know. He told me by next week, probably."

There are more nods and a grim silence that pushes Stephanie to finally say, "Listen, we can't leave this meeting on this note! I really do want to let you know how proud I am of all of you for how you pulled everything together in what was an unbelievably chaotic day. I really appreciate you all and please know I'm here to talk, too. I'm not a counselor, but I can listen. And I'll be back as soon as my leave is over."

She pauses. It might be in my head, but I swear I hear everyone groan. They want Stephanie back as soon as possible.

They want me gone.

"You all have my number. I'll talk about anything, anytime, and we'll get through this together."

Then I watch as Stephanie puts a big smile on her face. It might be my imagination, but as she looks at everyone in turn around the table, giving them her sure, confident, assuring smile, I swear she skips over me.

Kate—*After*

I hope Paul is awake as I return home from Robin's. Robin opened a bottle of wine when I sat down at her kitchen bar, and by the time I left, it was gone. We talked about everything. We talked about how I was coping. We talked about going to the funeral together Saturday. We talked about Bryan Price until I said I don't want to talk about it anymore.

In his usual fashion, Paul doesn't disappoint. I find him in the den, a beer in his hand, watching a game. The Lions. Heartbreakers. The volume's on low.

I sit down next to him and take the beer from his hand. His Labatt tastes thin after so much Cabernet. I buy the eight-dollar variety at Target, but Robin won't let a bottle into her home with a price tag less than twenty.

"Hey," Paul says playfully. "Get your own."

I hand the bottle back, smiling, watching him swirl it. "I'll get you another," I offer.

"Nah. It's late. We should go to bed."

I nod. "Kids asleep?"

"I think so. Last I checked, Kevin was finishing homework. But it's been quiet."

"Thanks for covering."

He shrugs off the thank you. It's an old habit: thanking each other for being the parent who stayed home so the other can go out. See a friend. Get a drink. Have a life. When the twins were younger, those social excursions were infrequent treasures. I suppose it isn't the same now that the kids are juniors in high school. Their needs have changed from one type of supervision to another.

Still, like all old habits, this one stuck.

"How's Robin?" he asks, taking another sip.

"She's fine." I think about expanding, but Paul's eyes are back on the television, watching a pass from the twenty-yard line come up short. I smile.

"And you?"

I sigh. I don't want to talk about Bryan Price anymore, but we will. "Tired, I suppose. I don't know. I think I'm feeling a little better. I just..."

He's looking at me thoughtfully. He doesn't know what to do with my sadness and confusion. But I know he doesn't like it. He lifts the beer to his lips, finishes it. "Come on, babe," he says. "Talk to me."

I recap everything Robin and I dissected. My best friend has been my sounding board for more than half my life. Between Robin and Paul, there isn't much I can't figure out. I tell him more about how Officer Dorsey interviewed me, how he'd brought up Madalynn. The thing about the snorkel, and how I carefully avoided telling Officer Dorsey my hangover was a big part of the reason I couldn't think straight that morning.

He's chuckling. It takes me a moment to process.

I sit up a little on the couch. "Are you laughing?"

"I'm sorry," he says. "I know it's not funny. It's just—the whole snorkel thing."

"What?"

"It's—I mean no disrespect."

"A man *died*, Paul."

"I know, I know." He puts his hands up in a defensive position. "It was sort of like, you know when you say a word enough times it loses its meaning? You've said snorkel like five times in a row, and it just strikes me what a silly word *snorkel* is."

I'm staring at him.

"Come on," he says. "Say it. *Snorkel. Snorkel. Snorkel.* It sounds like snoring. Or Urkel." He's grinning. "What a word. They couldn't have come up with a better word for that thing?"

My buzz is wearing off, but I must admit, he has a point. I smile.

On the screen, a quarterback for the other team throws a pass that a Lion tries to intercept. He drops it. I can read the lips of the head coach, to whom the camera immediately pans. He's swearing at another man holding a clipboard.

I remember that Bryan Price loved the Lions.

"A man *died*," I repeat. "And not just any man."

"I know." The smile disappears from his face. "Look, what can I say? I feel bad for him, I really do. I feel bad for his wife. That baby. But he shouldn't have signed up for a triathlon if he wasn't, you know, able to do one."

I frown. Paul hasn't said anything like this. He's been in protective mode. He's been helpful, understanding, picking up the slack. He's been doing my usual chores, taking care of dinner. Clean clothes have been magically appearing in our shared wardrobe for days. This is like the chink in his otherwise perfect armor.

"Maybe this isn't what you want to hear. I get that. But you know what? Babe, maybe I'm saying what you *need* to hear. You've been feeling responsible for Bryan's death. Maybe you need me to tell you—you know, or you need someone to tell you you're *not*!"

I look at him. He sets the empty beer bottle down.

"It's his own fault. He shouldn't have done a triathlon if he was such a weak swimmer that he needed a snorkel! There. I said it. Call me heartless."

Paul puts his arms out in a gesture meant to absolve him.

I take a breath, let it out. "Maybe." I close my eyes. "You're right about the whole, I feel responsible thing. But how could I *not* feel responsible? *I'm* the one who made the call that day, you know? It wasn't Stephanie. She would have made the right decision. But she wasn't there. It makes me sick to feel like all this could have been avoided if I'd, you know, not been too lazy to get my phone. If I'd taken the minute to text Stephanie. If I hadn't been so hungover. If I'd taken more time to think."

But Paul's shaking his head. "We've been over this," he says. We have.

"You had to make an on-the-spot decision. There wasn't time. The race was starting—the heat, or whatever. It was a gray area in the rules, and you know what? *You know what?* I'm not convinced Stephanie would have done the right thing. We'll never know what she would have done. Let's not play the hypothetical game. She might have made the exact same call. And then this would be on *her* head."

His voice is bitter now, like he's angry. I don't like it. I look back to the screen. The fourth quarter is ending. The Lions are about to lose.

"I don't mean, *on her head*. I don't mean to imply that this is on *your* head. Quite the opposite—that's the point of everything I'm trying to say." He softens. "I just don't like to see you feel so *responsible*. This was his choice—not yours. He wasn't a strong enough swimmer to do a triathlon and that's not your fault."

I don't admit this to Paul, but I'm still turning the word *snorkel* around in my head. It *does* sound silly. It sounds like a word a kid made up.

"Anyway," Paul says. I can tell he's winding down. "I know I'm a broken record. You made an on-the-spot decision for an event you were put in charge of, but you know what? No one put a gun to his head and made him exercise. Maybe he had a mid-life crisis, or whatever."

I consider. "Maybe. I mean, yeah. He wasn't athletic when I was with him. Maybe he did feel that pinch of getting older." I know that feeling well. "Why else do people do these kinds of things? Marathons, triathlons...isn't that the point? To feel young? Or to challenge yourself?"

"Mmm," Paul says. "Sure. But don't you think for Bryan, it was about showing *other* people he could it? I mean the guy was kind of a narcissist, wasn't he? From what you told me? And—you know. Because of…the thing."

Paul doesn't want to mention the ultimatum that ended my first marriage. But he knows about it. All he needs to do is gesture toward it and I fill in the blanks.

"Maybe."

"He shouldn't have signed up for an event that was too difficult for him. It was his pride. Did any of the other swimmers bring snorkels? Ask to use them?"

I shake my head. It had just been Bryan.

"In all the years you've *gone* to the event, have you ever seen a swimmer use a snorkel?"

I shake my head again. Never.

Paul sits back a little on the couch like a defense attorney resting his case. Which, I figure, he has. "Come on, babe. Let's go to bed. We lost. As usual."

Madalynn—*After*

There's no way the woman who just walked in the door carrying a hobo bag is who I think it is. If I hadn't been on my way back from the bathroom where a woman let me cut in line, I would have punched Kate Barkway again.

From the corner of my eye, I watch her take a seat with her friend in one of the back pews. Good. At least she knows her place, but why is she here at all? Her ex-husband's funeral?

I sit next to Ginger, there with her husband, until they shift, insist I sit between Mom and Dad. I want to tell my sister who I just saw, but a fresh batch of sobs takes over. As much as I want to spit out the words, I can only put my head on her shoulder and cry.

Ginger offers me a handkerchief and I feel my dad's strong hand on my shoulder. I focus on my breathing and the sound of the instrumental piano music playing over the speakers. The funeral is supposed to start any minute now.

Reverend Hadleigh might even be waiting for me to compose myself before he begins, I realize. Everything around me feels simultaneously quiet and far too loud—the music, the whispers, the footsteps on the hardwood floor, the shuffling of the bodies as everyone sits down.

I would say I couldn't believe how many people were here at Bryan's funeral—except I *could* believe it. Everyone loves Bryan. *Loved.* I start crying harder. Reverend Hadleigh is up to the podium—lectern—whatever it's called. With my dad's handkerchief, I dab at my eyes and examine the white cloth for evidence of black mascara. None. Good.

"Good morning," Reverend Hadleigh begins. There's a murmur of *good morning* in return from the mourners.

I shift my weight in the pew to get a little more comfortable. The baby is sitting like a bowling ball on my bladder. I felt her kicking earlier and for a while after my mother forced me to drink a whole glass of orange juice.

Truthfully, most of the mornings since it happened have been a blur: my mom knocking on the bathroom door when I've been in the shower for twenty minutes, crying. The dress she found for me—maternity. Is there anything more depressing than a black maternity dress? It's an awful polyester blend, empire waste. Long-sleeved. Not my style whatsoever, but there my mom was, helping me zip it up.

This is the same church Bryan and I got married in, just a few years ago. Almost three. Does anyone sitting in this room know that?

Many of the people at the funeral were at our wedding. I shake with a fresh sob.

"We're here to celebrate the life of Bryan Price," I hear.

And then honestly, all the words out of Reverend Hadleigh's mouth become one long stream I'm unable to follow. It's another language. My dad takes my hand, holding it tight, and when I finally feel like I can look at him without sobbing, I do. His face is sober. There are wrinkles on his tan skin. As best I can with a thirty-pound belly, I lean into my mom and let out a wail so loud, Reverend Hadleigh pauses for a second and coughs before continuing.

I stare at the large picture of Bryan someone framed. It's a photo from our wedding—a portrait of Bryan the photographer had taken right before we did our first pictures.

There are Bible verses—I know that.

There are songs. Hymns.

When everyone stands to sing, I stay planted in my seat. Ginger and my mom hold my hands. Halfway through the second song, I feel like I have to pee again, but there's no way I'm going to walk by everyone, let them see my blotchy face, my red eyes. Particularly not Kate. The eulogies start and Bryan's mother speaks, and then his father, then his sister. His friends William and Andy get up to talk, too. I feel everyone's eyes staring at the back of my head.

If anyone thinks I'm going to talk, they are in for disappointment. In my stomach, the baby decides to have a dance party right when I think there's no way I have enough fluid in my body for more tears, I start to cry all over again. Dad and Mom are on either side of me. *It's time to go*, one of them says. They each take one of my arms and divide the weight of my body between them.

It's time to bury Bryan. I want to scream. I can't believe this is happening.

Why did this go by so fast? Shouldn't more people say something?

The more people talk, the longer we can delay what's next—what Mr. Sheldon, the humorless funeral director had walked me through in his office with Mom and Dad flanking me yesterday—or was that two days ago? I can't remember. I can't remember anything except that I haven't gone to work, and I've been sleeping on Bryan's side of the bed, and my mom drove me to my prenatal appointment, where I cried the whole time, alarming all the other pregnant women in the waiting room until my mother whispered to each of them in turn, *she just lost her husband*, as a way to explain I wasn't out of control because of anything wrong with the baby.

At least there was nothing wrong with the baby.

I still had the baby—a girl. We were planning to name her Isabelle. Bella for short.

At least I still had Bella.

She was half of Bryan.

That's what everyone was thinking, wasn't it?

He was so young. He'd just gotten married! Just discovered he was going to be a father.

What a loss for the community. What a loss for the family.

He was a good man, he was a great man, he was a wonderful man.

Look, there she is, they were whispering. Poor thing. She looks like she's about to pop.

Won't it be so hard to do it alone, but at least she still has the baby. Still. What a shame. Bryan would have made an excellent father.

And Kate Barkway has the audacity to show up at his funeral?

I can't stand it. I shoot her a look as I walk by her—her and her ugly, gray-haired friend. She should really lose some weight. Kate—not the friend. The friend is slim, not unattractive. Kate's face is full and puffy and haggard. She doesn't have the balls to look at me when I pass. Good.

If she looks at me, I feel like I'll turn her to stone, like Medusa. My dad is telling me it's time. As unbelievable as it is, it's time to put Bryan in the ground.

If there hadn't been eight people in the pew between us, I might have reached out and punched Kate Barkway in her fat face this time.

Kate—*After*

From several pews away, I make out the sound of Madalynn Price sobbing.

The service is about to begin. I exchange a glance with Robin, glad that she hadn't needed much convincing to drive all the way to Rockford with me. I don't want Paul here. I want to shield Paul from this. I want to be here without Paul as my shield, like it's a crime to show up at my ex-husband's funeral with my current husband.

He'd seemed relieved—happy to eschew the obligation, the occasion to wear a dark suit and sit in a room with strangers.

I can't be sure, but I feel people pointing at me. There's a woman in the second pew whispering to a man, and I swear I hear *Kate* escape her lips. Are they wondering why I'm here? Is anyone saying this was my fault? I strain to listen, but I can't make out words.

Looking around, I see Bryan's parents sitting near Madalynn. They'd remember me, wouldn't they? His sister, too. My extra pounds aside, I don't look that dissimilar from my old self. I decide then to skip the burial. The last thing I want is a conversation with Bryan's family. Or with Madalynn.

The reverend begins to speak. I feel weirdly numb. His voice makes this funeral feel uncomfortably and undeniably real.

I look over at Robin, but she's staring straight ahead. I'm thankful she didn't say it was weird I wanted to come. She'd only asked what time I'd like to be picked up.

I look down and read the obituary printed under Bryan's color photo. Then I reread it. It's longer than the one I saw posted online. I'd seen that yesterday. Robin had sent me the link, although she hadn't needed to.

There's no mention of me in that obituary—of our lives together. I'm still thinking about that. Those months we spent as newlyweds in that small apartment. The good times. There were good times, weren't there? When we were dating. When we were engaged. That first Christmas: snowed in for a weekend, watching movies and baking frozen pizzas. That trip to the Upper Peninsula where we never put in a CD because we talked the whole way. A birthday party for a mutual friend.

There were good times. Maybe my name shouldn't be in his obituary, but shouldn't my contribution to his life be recognized in some way? Shouldn't I have more of a connection to the day than a dirty look from Madalynn Price?

But this obituary is printed neatly on the back of the folded cream paper. All that text: the bare bones of his life under a color photo. Birthdate. Birthplace. Parents. Education. Career. Wife. Hobbies. His whole life, summarized in three hundred words. I'm not even a footnote. My name has no place here.

But I also know that that doesn't mean I had no place in his life. I was part of his story. He was part of mine. His obituary *could* have included, "briefly married to Kate Turner…" or "after a short marriage to Kate Turner…" No. That was all stupid. It was right that my name isn't there in black and white. Kate Turner? I barely remember that person. It wasn't too long after we divorced that I met Paul, became Kate Barkway. It was like when a dog is adopted from a kennel and the new owners change its name—decide it's more of a Stanley than a Hans. That was me.

If someone called out, "Kate Turner"—or "Kate Price"—I wouldn't turn around for either of those names anymore.

No. I decide then it's right that Madalynn Price is his only real wife. Most of the people in this room have no idea who I am. That's right.

I should let myself get erased from his life, even if Madalynn and God knows who else thinks I had something to do with his death.

Let everyone erase me from his life.

Erase me from his death, too.

Madalynn—*After*

I can't sleep. I sit on the couch with my laptop, in the dark. I can't stop reading about people who have died during triathlons. I have a dozen websites bookmarked and a bunch of academic articles downloaded.

Did you know that according to a study commissioned by USA Triathlon between 2003 and 2011, forty-four athletes died in sanctioned events? The study also concluded that most deaths occurred in or directly after the swim portion.

Not a surprise! The swim portion is the most difficult.

Did you know people have died doing the Ironman?

I guess that shouldn't surprise anyone either.

Bryan was no Ironman, but he'd done the training for the triathlon.

How many mornings did he get up at 4:30 to get to the YMCA to swim his laps before work? How many after-dinner jogs did he do?

The joke around our house was that he'd better get his training in now. After our baby was born, no way was he going to have the time or the energy.

Women nest. Bryan checked an item off his bucket list.

And I was so proud of him.

Every time he'd come back from a bike ride sweating.

Every time he went to bed at 8:30 p.m. so he could get up early the next day.

The calendar he kept in the kitchen marking his training plan. He'd started in April. Those neat boxes filled with crossed-out days and notes on his time and activities.

While my body grew our baby, his body grew in strength. The transformation was incredible. Bryan was a lot older than me, sure, but suddenly, he had the body of someone ten years younger. I teased him about getting hot right when I was getting fat, but he'd only ever reassured me I looked beautiful—pregnant and all.

God, I miss his body—that body. His smile. I miss him so fucking much.

I have the Wikipedia page practically memorized. A litany of depressing statistics.

Yes, "List of Triathlon Fatalities" is a real page on Wikipedia.

It took me some failed searches to find it, but I had a feeling someone curated such a list and kept it up to date. I couldn't be the only person fascinated and horrified. The data went back to 1986. Nearly two hundred names. Bryan's hasn't been added yet. I wonder if I should do it.

My eyes swim over the words, the causes of their deaths.

Heart attack.

Struck by vehicle on the course.

Slammed into a guard rail at the bottom of a hill.

Collapsed on the run.

One even said *Unnatural Death*. No link to check at the bottom of the Wikipedia page. I have no idea what that means.

According to a recent study, the injuries that required medical attention include broken bones, heat exhaustion, dehydration, and hypothermia.

I Google, *If someone dies in a triathlon can you sue*?

That brings me to a page about someone suing over the death of a marathoner. I find a forum online detailing how a wrongful death suit was brought against USA Triathlon. The first comment discusses insurance: a quarter million dollars. Does the city of East Grand Rapids have insurance?

And *that much*? How much could I sue for, if I *could* sue?

I stare at my belly. Couldn't we *use* the money?

I did okay, salary-wise, but the funeral expenses were going to be in the thousands, and now I was going to need to live on just my income. Still waiting to hear how much I'd get from Bryan's life insurance.

I read on.

One website says at least three lawsuits have been filed against event organizers. Those suits cited unsafe race conditions, that they had neglected safety measures. That there hadn't been enough safety personnel. Were there enough safety personnel the day Bryan died? I squeeze my eyes shut asking my brain to recall how many lifeguards there had been. I can't remember.

According to one article, the popularity of endurance sports is growing. There are more than 4,300 triathlons annually around the United States. This figure only counts officially sanctioned races. I guess this one was officially sanctioned. I mean, this one is reputable. I make a mental note to go back to the website and look for that information later.

I can't stop thinking about how Bryan had done everything right. He'd trained. He'd eaten well. He'd lost thirty pounds. He'd watched videos on YouTube, shopped Amazon for the right gear. He'd done every single thing right. It wasn't fair that he was dead.

Could I sue for not allowing him to have that fucking snorkel? He'd trained with it the whole time. He expected to use it. He must have looked up the rules. He would have known.

Could I sue Kate?

I'd have to sue the city. The department. Right? Would a lawyer even take my case? Wrongful death, or—should I be citing one of these specific things? There should have been more lifeguards. Response time from the city should have been faster? Some of the cases have gone to federal court.

I have no idea what I'm doing, but that doesn't stop me from Googling.

Personal injury lawyers? Every site I visit comes with a pop up encouraging me to contact someone *right now*.

It's not like Kate Barkway has millions, even if I do sue her. Does she? Maybe. According to Zillow, her house is worth a fair amount. Nothing in my Googling, however, leads me to conclude I can sue her personally. Everything I'm reading tells me the waiver he signed is the most critical thing.

Then it occurs to me.

I've never seen the waiver. Bryan signed up online. What the hell did it say?

I open a new tab and navigate to the city's page. I find the 20th annual Charles E. Belknap Legacy Triathlon page.

My breath catches in my throat.

There, on the page, is a picture of Bryan. The portrait we used for his obituary. And there's his obituary. I start sobbing. Someone—Kate?—changed the information page about the race to *this*. I don't know whether to thank them or hate them, so I sob loud sobs. I go to the site to find a link to the register, but of course, it's not there. The event is over.

Mom comes into the living room to find me a heaping mess on my couch.

"Madalynn," Mom is saying. "It's after midnight. I think you should put the computer away and get some rest. Honey, you need to sleep."

No. What I need is to get my hands on that fucking waiver.

* * *

It's just after ten a.m. when Officer Dorsey knocks on my door.

Not that his visit is a surprise.

He'd called Thursday and said he'd like to talk—but only after Bryan's funeral. He wanted to respect my space and give me time to get through the funeral first.

What a nice guy to not make the pregnant widow come down

to Public Safety, particularly considering Public Safety shares a parking lot with Parks and Recreation. With my luck, I'd run into Kate Barkway returning from a donut run.

How is it possible that I've gone years without ever having to see my husband's ex-wife in person, and suddenly she's every-*fucking*-where. At the race. At his funeral.

In Bryan's inbox.

Yeah, I saw that. Bryan and I keep our passwords in a shared app. Total trust.

I logged into his account a few days after his passing to make his account a memorial page. I could see people were writing on his wall, and so one afternoon when I had the energy, I thought I'd take care of that. Just one tiny thing on my list of things to do.

Honestly, I can't believe how much there is to do. I have to update everything: health insurance; car insurance; our Verizon plan. Thank God I was able to swap over to my insurance without an issue. I don't know how I'm expected in the thick of grief to do all the things I've had to. Thank God Mom is still staying here, in the guest room.

Which is between our room and the nursery.

When Officer Dorsey comes over, though, Mom's at the store. I didn't tell her he was coming. I didn't want her to feel like she had to hang around.

"Come in," I say. He's dressed in a dark uniform, holding a hat on top of a black portfolio. Honestly, why do East Grand Rapids Public Safety officers dress like real cops? They totally aren't. Nickers, our corgi, barks.

"Can I get you anything? Coffee? Water?"

"I'm fine, thank you. I'm sorry for your loss."

I nod. He already said it on the phone—twice. I gesture he should sit on the beige couch across from me. I'm glad now Mom spent some time tidying yesterday—dusting, running the vacuum, putting away clothes and dishes. I'd told her at first to stop it, but she said a clean house would make me feel better. It was kind of her, but honestly, nothing is making me feel better. I can't even drink. I'd kill for tequila. Instead, it's a decaf tea in my hand as I pull my oversized cardigan over my belly.

"How are you?" he asks evenly.

"Fine," I answer. He might be asking about my pregnancy or my grief. I don't want to talk about either. I've only cried once this morning. "Yourself?"

He nods but doesn't look at me. He's opening his black portfolio and taking out a folder.

"I have the results of Bryan's autopsy, and I'd like to go over them with you."

I'm not sure if he's going to hand the folder over, so I just stare at him. I sniffle. He clears his throat.

"I'm sure this continues to be very difficult for you, Mrs. Price." He reads from the manilla folder. "The results do conclude that the cause of death for Bryan was laryngospasm and pulmonary injury, resulting in hypoxemia and acidosis." He pauses to study me.

I nod.

"Additionally, Bryan suffered from cardiac arrest."

I don't know why, but it hits me like a gut punch. "He did?"

Officer Dorsey nods. "It's the coroner's opinion that"—he glances at the paper in front of him—"that the hypoxia is the result of the lack of oxygen. So yes, the cardiac arrest was brought on by the drowning."

I sit still for a long moment. "Bryan drowned, *then* he had a heart attack?"

He nods.

"He just… *first*, he drowned?"

He nods again. "Yes. He was overcome in the water, and that strain led to cardiac arrest."

I don't know what to say. I can't believe he just literally drowned. That his lungs filled up with water. That he couldn't breathe. I squeeze my eyes shut.

"I'm sorry," I whisper.

"It's all right," he says softly.

"Why didn't the scuba divers save him?" I whisper. It's a question I'd already asked everyone, and I already know the answer.

The look on his face is sympathetic. "Unfortunately, they were unable to get to him in time."

I hate that phrase: in time.

We're always *in* time. We're never able to be *outside* of time. We're always just stuck in it, for better or worse.

I'm crying hard.

Officer Dorsey pauses. "I'm so sorry. Do you want to see the report?"

I nod. He hands me the folder, but honestly, the words on the paper swim in front of my eyes, and I just pretend to read. I see Bryan's full name, the date, the one-sentence summary typed in italics. The words *hypoxia* and *acidosis* pop up on the page at me. There's a diagram of a body left totally blank, and that's what pushes me to sobs. Bryan is now a body. Just a body. A body we put in the ground three days ago. A body that isn't coming home. A body that won't hold me, kiss me, make love with me.

And a body that will never hold his child.

I feel the cushion next to me sink down. A moment later, I feel Officer Dorsey's hand on my shoulder. "I'm so sorry," he says again. He takes the report out of my hand.

"I guess I just—" I sob. "I don't know," I manage to get out. In my nose, I feel snot gathering. I am ugly crying. I reach over for a tissue and blow. "I guess I just thought this report would say something else."

He nods. I'm not sure what I've said makes sense, but he acts like it does. After he gives me a moment, he takes his hand off my shoulder.

"With the results of the autopsy complete, my department is ready to conclude our report. But if you have additional questions or think of anything else you can still reach out to me."

"That's it?"

He nods. "Yes."

"And just… nothing happens to *her*?"

He frowns. "Who?"

"His ex-wife." It comes out in a hiss. I don't want to say her name. I hate her name. I hate that she had his name for a time. "Nothing happens to *her*?" And even as the words come out of my mouth, they sound stupid. Now all I want to hear is the sound of the garage door opening, my mother coming in with an armful of brown paper grocery sacks. "She was in charge of the race."

He hesitates. "I've spoken with Ms. Barkway. The cause of death is under no suspicion."

"I know," I say, rolling my eyes. "He signed that waiver. I just—the snorkel thing. Bryan trained with a snorkel the whole time and then, you know, it's the day *of* and she tells him he can't have it." I'm not telling him anything he doesn't already know. It doesn't move the needle.

"I see," he nods.

He thinks I'm a hysterical woman. I don't care. There's *some* way she's responsible. I just feel it, even if I can't prove it.

"She told him he couldn't have the one thing he needed," I say, my voice low. "She would have *known* he needed it."

He considers. "Ms. Barkway disallowed that equipment for *all* swimmers."

I can't tell if he's asking or stating. He looks like he wants to add something, but he doesn't.

"She told him he couldn't have it," I repeat.

"She didn't single him out. According to her assistant, she only knew the number of the racer who was inquiring—not the name."

"No one else asked," I say.

He shrugs. I wonder if he's ever investigated an actual murder before.

"She's his ex-wife," I remind him, as though that in and of itself is some kind of crime.

"There appears to have been no—you know, differentiated treatment for Mr. Price, in terms of his participation in this event. I don't think it was personal."

This isn't getting me anywhere. I don't know how to make him see her culpability.

Then, like lightning, a thought strikes in my mind. I whip my cell phone out of the pocket of my sweater. He's watching me. "Here," I say. I log out of my Facebook account so I can log into Bryan's. "Take a look at what she said to him."

I watch Officer Dorsey squint at my phone. I should have offered to get Bryan's tablet, but he frowns and hands the phone back to me before I can.

"Did you read it?" I ask.

Nice to see you changed your mind.

He nods, slowly, frowns. "I did."

"Isn't that weird? She sent it *after* he died. I mean, why would she *do* that?"

He shakes his head again.

Her message had been short, yet so cryptic.

Bryan hadn't even been friends with her on Facebook. I'd seen the red dot indicating a message request and honestly, just as easily could have missed it. In fact, part of me wished I *had* missed it. But of course I saw it, and in between reading hundreds of supportive message from friends who care about me and about Bryan, I had to be confronted with this psychotic message from his ex-wife.

What the actual fuck.

Officer Dorsey isn't saying anything, so I press. "I mean did you look at the date on that message? She sent it the day *after* he died."

He nods.

"Isn't that weird?"

He nods again. "It is odd."

I ask Officer Dorsey, "What do you think it means?"

He frowns. "I'm afraid I don't know. At first I thought you were saying that she'd said something to him about the snorkel. But she sent this after? So, it can't be that."

I nod. *Some detective you are*, I think.

I hate, too, that Kate can tell I read that message. It makes my skin crawl. I wonder if she expects me to respond.

"So, you're saying, or you're asking, why did she send this message to Bryan, knowing he had already passed? I don't have an answer for that. What do you think?"

He's asked it gently—this question, carefully talking me through this.

But I've already given the question a lot of thought. Of course I have. It's been burning into my brain.

Changed his mind about *what*?

Had he said he would never remarry, or something? That was possible. He certainly waited a long time to remarry. He used to joke with me that he'd resigned himself to a life of perpetual bachelorhood, but one look at me had changed all that.

Maybe when they were splitting up, they'd had a conversation about that. Or a fight. Maybe he'd told her he didn't want kids at all. That was possible. When I told Bryan I wanted to start our family right away, he was a little gun-shy. It took me a few months to warm him up to the idea—convince him he wasn't too old. That it wasn't too late.

I shake my head and say, "She came to his funeral. Did you know that? I just think that's so weird. And suspicious."

He nods, considering. "She *is* his ex-wife. Perhaps she's processing it, too."

I roll my eyes.

How dare he, I yell inside my head.

"Bryan had nothing to do with her. He hadn't spoken to her in, like, twenty years, or whatever."

But Officer Dorsey shrugs again and gives me a look like I'm too young to understand.

"If I were you," he says, "and if I may dispense some—some fatherly advice, I would just ignore Ms. Barkway."

This time I'm unable to resist the urge to roll my eyes.

Like she's harmless? I think. I don't think so.

Whatever. He's no help. He thinks I'm being crazy.

I'm not being crazy. And I'm not dumb. I always understand more than people think I do. It's because I'm pretty. I know. People have always treated me like that, my whole life—like they're surprised when I graduated at the top of my class. Surprised I carried a perfect 4.0 in college. Surprised I landed my job as the Director of Marketing when I was only twenty-six.

Surprised I could be pretty *and* smart, I guess. Like because I'm pretty, I don't need to have a lot going on upstairs.

Guess what?

I do.

Kate—*After*

I keep having the same dream. I've had it three times now.

Sometimes I wake up at four in the morning panting like I've just run up a hill. I reach for Paul, then, press my face against his bicep in bed. I do it carefully, so I don't wake him. He's been tending to me so much, I don't want to make him tend to me in his sleep.

In the dream—in every dream—Bryan Price is drowning. And I'm drowning, too.

The word *drowning* starts to inhabit every sense of time, and me along with it. I did drown. I am drowning. I will drown. I'm about to drown.

Drown, drown, drown, drown, drown.

Weeds. Dark black waves, undulating, pulling, pushing.

I try to move my arms, swim toward the shore, but where is it?

Which way is up? I can't breathe. I can't move. My limbs are cement—dead and cold and immovable. I can't see anything. At my feet, on my shins, all the way up to my knees, I feel the weeds pulling, grasping, sucking me down, down, down, under, under, under.

I can make out a face in front of me: a flesh-colored blob whose familiar features arrange themselves in a configuration I know all too well.

I don't understand why he's in the water with me.

I don't understand why we are drowning together.

Kate, he cries, moving his lips. I can't hear his voice clearly in the water, but I know what he's saying just the same: *Help me.*

* * *

A man in a blue coat is flying a kite with a young boy. It's mesmerizing. I study the boy as he jumps up and down at his father's feet. The boy's arms reach for the string. Three times already, the kite has fallen from the air the moment the dad handed over the string. I find myself wishing for the boy's sake he would just let his father keep it. Why can't he leave well enough alone, and just enjoy the sight of the kite dancing in the breeze?

A knock on Stephanie's door brings me to attention. Chelsea. She's holding her laptop in her arm, folded open.

"Come in."

She sets the laptop down, then turns its screen toward me. "I'm assuming you've seen this."

Unfortunately, yes. Robin sent me the link an hour ago.

"How many signatures is she up to?"

She frowns. "Twenty-seven? Oh. Whoops. Twenty-eight. Sorry."

"Wow. That many people want me to get fired. That's... something."

Chelsea grimaces. "I doubt she'll reach her goal. And even if she does, it's not like Stephanie's actually going to fire you."

"Right," I say slowly.

Chelsea shrugs. "Anyway, I just came in here to see if you were okay. I think she's just, you know, posturing. Putting on a show."

"She literally started a Change.org petition to get me fired."

"I know," Chelsea says. "She's grieving. And trying to get attention."

"I feel like this story's had enough attention." I say it softly even though it's just the two of us.

Chelsea nods. "I know. I wish this would all go away. And—no offense—I can't wait for Stephanie to return."

Me either, I think. "You think she's seen this?"

Chelsea shrugs. "She hasn't said anything. I don't want you to worry. This petition—even if she gets the five hundred signatures, that's not how it works."

"Maybe I should quit."

"No," Chelsea says immediately. "Don't you dare."

But she doesn't sound one hundred percent sincere—at least not to me.

I look back out the window at the lakeshore. The kite is back in the air. I can see the tail ties flapping in the breeze. It's supposed to be something—a shape. A dragon? It could have horns, a tail, a flame.

I say, "I'm sure what she wants is her husband back. She thinks I murdered him."

Chelsea looks at me and doesn't say anything. "If there's blame to be shared, then I'm a murderer, too."

"What are you talking about?"

Chelsea has tears in her eyes. "*I* didn't know the rule. *I* could have known. *I* could have checked Stephanie's binder—or called her. Texted her. But I didn't do any of that. I just asked *you*. I didn't take any responsibility."

"It was *my* call," I assure her. "You didn't do anything wrong." It's sweet she's protecting me. In the time since Bryan's death, I've scoured Stephanie's binder. There's nothing in there about snorkels. I tell her so.

"I came in here to make *you* feel better. Which, by the way:

donuts in the break room."

I stand and follow her to the door. "Next time there's a petition to get me fired, please lead with the good news."

Kate—*After*

I'm staring at the lake again. Half a dozen boats bob on the water. It's Friday. This hellish week is finally almost over. Tomorrow is Saturday. I can sleep in, read the paper in bed with Paul. Have coffee and croissants. Feel normal.

I'm clinging to that thought like it's a life raft.

Chelsea's at my door again, and I frown. We don't have a meeting. I've barely done any work since the triathlon, but everyone seems to be giving me space. Luke hasn't been in all week. I've spent most of the time looking out Stephanie's window at the water.

"Someone's here to see you," Chelsea says.

"Oh. Sure."

"It's Madalynn Price."

At first, I'd worried it was someone from MLive. I'd directed them to Stephanie the first two times, but someone had followed up yesterday and it had put me on edge. There were a few feature pieces on Bryan, and someone wanted a quote from me for an article about the donations. Stephanie had organized a press release diverting the proceeds from the race to Madalynn Price instead of the Historical Society. The Society was fine with it. Apparently, there'd been an out-pouring of support. A lot of money getting donated.

A lot of money.

I hope it's enough to make Madalynn Price drop this petition to get me fired.

I clear my throat then look to the door. Then there's Madalynn's face.

She looks amazing. She's wearing a navy shirt dress. It floats over her belly in the most flattering way. She's got her hair pulled back into a sleek ponytail, her blonde bangs neatly brushed to one side. Even her shoes are cute. I never wear heels—and certainly didn't when I was carrying Krista and Keith. But there she is in nude pumps, looking red-carpet ready. I'm distracted for a second by her tan legs.

"I'll make this fast," she says. "I'm here because I want to see the waiver Bryan signed. *Please.*"

"Oh. Sure. Come on in."

Funny we've skipped right over the introductions. I suppose there's no need when you're fully aware who the other person is.

I look in the top right drawer of the desk for Stephanie's binder. I can't recall if there's a copy of the waiver in it. Registration has been done fully online the last three or four years, so it may or may not be printed and three-hole punched.

I'm aware she's staring at me, her arms crossed over her belly. I stop.

"Madalynn," I say, looking up from my search. "I just want to say I'm so sorry about—"

"Nope," she interrupts. "I don't want to talk to you. I just want the waiver. I looked online, but I couldn't find it. Do you have it?"

She stares at me for another long moment. I wonder if I should invite her to sit down, since she's so pregnant. But I do not want her to stay any longer than she has to; I suspect she doesn't want to, either.

Finally, in the binder, I spy what I'm looking for. I don't bother to open the three-ring binder. Instead, I just rip the two pages out like an animal. I hand them to Madalynn Price.

"This is last year's. I don't think I printed this year's, but I am sure it's the same. The only thing that would have changed is the date."

"I *need* this year's," she insists, although she takes the pages from my hand. She must think this is better than nothing. It's a lot to take from the woman who started a petition to get me fired. I don't know what she thinks she's going to prove.

"Okay," I say. "Send me an email. My address is on our site. I'll find this year's waiver and email it to you. Is there anything else I can do?"

"No," she says. "I'll expect the correct waiver as soon as possible." She looks like she wants to say something else, but she just goes to the door, pages in her hand.

I say *of course*. She walks out of Stephanie's office. As she walks out, I think about telling her I know she read my message to Bryan. I noticed the word "seen" next to it.

Either that, or my ex-husband has found a way to log in to Facebook from beyond the grave.

I'd half expected her to bring it up, but I know I barely know this woman. I don't know what their marriage was really like. I don't even know how they met. I only know what I know from Facebook—the stuff Robin made sure I saw when she figured out the two of them were having a baby. I don't know what made her want to marry a man old enough to be her father.

Part of me doesn't know why Robin would even remember anything about my marriage to Bryan—it was so long ago. I've remarried, had children, raised them. My marriage to Bryan Price feels like a planet in another solar system.

Yet my best friend occasionally cyber stalks my ex-husband and his new picture-perfect, Instagram-worthy wife, and sends me screenshots with snarky captions.

Part of me wants to say, I don't know why Robin holds on to any hard feelings about Bryan Price, given how long ago all this transpired, given how much we've all moved on.

But part of me knows.

Robin remembers.

She hasn't forgiven him for what he did, either.

Kate—*Before*

The instructions on the box were simple enough. Even though I had no reason to feel like a delinquent buying it at the drugstore, I did. I'd never bought one before.

Now, as I sat on the bathroom floor staring at the stick I just peed on, I felt…

I wasn't sure what I was feeling. I wasn't sure what I was supposed to feel. I just stared at the stick, numbly, waiting for what was going to come next.

What's the expression? A watched pot doesn't brew? I stared at the small white circle in which I was certain I saw a thin, pink line emerging.

I took a deep breath, trying to think about either outcome.

If it's negative, no problem. I'll have wasted nine bucks. No one will even know. I'll have a good laugh. Maybe I'll tell Robin. She'll laugh as well.

If it's positive…

That would explain why I'm late. Why I've been so tired.

Oh my God. That second pink line was becoming clear.

Oh my God. I picked up the test. I didn't care that it'd been peed on, I held it to my face.

Oh my God. No way. This couldn't be happening.

But there it was, plain as day. It hadn't taken five minutes, as the box had said. But who was I going to tell that to? Robin? Would I go back to the drug store and tell the clerk who'd checked me out that the product misidentified its timeframe for results delivery?

I felt sick.

I couldn't blink. Those lines weren't going anywhere, were they? Twin lines. Twin pink lines. They looked strong, defiant. So certain of themselves. Two little lines that were going to change my life forever.

I was so absorbed in staring at the test that I didn't hear the apartment door unlock. I didn't hear the door shut. I was still sitting on the cold white tile, holding the stick when I heard my name, and *what are you doing?*

Finally, I looked up at my husband's face.

"What's the matter?"

"You're never going to believe this. Oh my God. Bryan, I'm pregnant."

* * *

Bryan's face was giving me no clues. What it was giving me was anxiety.

"How did this happen?" he demanded. I wondered if he noticed I was still sitting on the bathroom floor—that I was still holding that stupid pregnancy stick. Test. I wanted him to want to sit down beside. Was that too much to ask? I wished he would say something else.

"I don't know," I said.

Because I honestly didn't. I wasn't lying to Bryan.

We'd only been married a month. We hadn't waited until the wedding to have sex. We hadn't spent our honeymoon in bed, per se, but that was also because we were too broke to do much. We'd had a grand, a little less—enough to drive to the Upper Peninsula for a few days. Hike Tahquamenon Falls. Buy some souvenirs.

Robin didn't believe we'd spent our honeymoon being careful. We'd been careful. I'd tried to remember to take my pill at the same time every day.

Had I missed one?

This couldn't be happening.

Bryan sighed. His arms were crossed. He was still wearing his work clothes: khaki pants and a blue button down. He hated his IT job, but I hated my job as a store manager, too. This wasn't exactly our plan. The pieces were slowly clicking together in my mind. He's mad, I realized. He's angry. He's actually…pissed as hell.

Bryan is furious at me for being pregnant.

My new husband. Brand new.

"Aren't you on the pill?" His tone indicated he thought I was stupid. His tone let me know this was all my fault—a mistake born out of my own stupidity. Not his.

I frowned. "I am! I mean, it isn't perfect but…"

Mentally I scanned the last two cycles—the last two months. Had I fucked it up? Maybe in the stress of moving to our apartment together, planning our tiny wedding and tiny honeymoon…maybe I'd missed one. Or two.

This felt like a nightmare. All I wanted was to rewind back to the morning—before my trip to CVS, before I took this test, before anything was wrong. I just wanted to rewind everything. I wanted to pretend none of this is happening.

And I wanted Bryan to comfort me. I wanted him to sit by me and understand I was upset, too. That I hadn't meant for this to happen.

That this hadn't been some kind of trick—nothing I'd done on purpose.

I wouldn't do something like this on purpose. I wasn't a bad person. I was a good person—didn't he know that?

"Dammit Kate," he said. His fingers were in his hair. "We are *not* having a baby. I'm *not* ready to be a father. Goddammit. I really wish…"

He let his voice trail off. Part of me wanted to keep the silence, hang it like a wreath in the air. Silence felt good. Silence felt like he wasn't going to yell at me.

"You really wish what?" I asked, despite myself.

"I really wish you hadn't let this happen."

I let this happen, he'd said.

"Are you going to take care of it?" That was the next thing out of his mouth. His arms were still folded across his chest. He still looked mad enough to spit.

Take care of it.

"Take care of what?"

He looked at me then like I was an idiot.

We were two months into our marriage, and he was looking at me like I was the dumbest person he'd ever met—dumber than the clients he helped on the phone who can't figure out how to connect a modem. I heard about them all the time.

"You've got to take care of this pregnancy. You gotta, you know. Get *it* taken care of."

My brain was catching up. My butt was getting cold on the tile. I just wanted this exchange to be over. I just wanted to crawl into bed. I wanted to call my mother, too, but I knew on this one, I couldn't.

"You want me to get an abortion," I whispered.

"Ding ding ding," he said sarcastically.

Then he scoffed and walked away. I studied his backside as he walked down the hall to our shitty kitchen. Then, I looked down at my stomach—my belly.

Of course I didn't see anything. It was nothing yet.

But in that moment, I knew there was no way I could.

* * *

I don't tell anyone for a long time.

I move in with Shannon, a college friend. We had a slew of classes together, and she got a job right after graduation that paid her well enough to get an apartment with two bedrooms. Her spare room becomes my refuge.

To Shannon, I admit that Bryan and I are having problems. She's sweet and understanding. She's never met Bryan, and she's so busy with her job, she keeps to herself and lets me do the same. I'm so grateful for her kindness, I don't have the words.

Bryan won't let me come home until I agree to the abortion. I'm not allowed, he tells me, to come home until I'm no longer pregnant. He says it's simple: come home when I'm no longer pregnant.

I lose my job because I call in sick too many times in a row. I'm not sick, exactly. I know I could play the pregnancy card—cite morning sickness. The regional manager, Beth, actually likes me. She has two kids. She'd understand.

Instead, she fires me regretfully over the phone over my attendance and sounds really sad about it. The whole conversation, I think about how I could tell her and how she'd give me my position back in a heartbeat; I have the feeling, too, that if I tell her what Bryan told me, she'd be on my side. She'd tell me to leave him.

Who forces his wife to have an abortion?

But I tell no one.

Which makes it easier a few weeks later when I lose the pregnancy.

I'm at the mall when it happens—of all places. A gush of blood. A woman points at my jeans, alerting me. She's concerned. I find a restroom. The woman tells me I should get to a doctor. She calls an ambulance for me. The ambulance picks me up outside the food court. A lot of people are staring. I feel silly, but I also feel scared. I am pretty sure I understand I've miscarried, but I want a kind doctor in a white coat to tell me.

And then to tell me everything is going to be all right.

Which is what happens. I stay at Shannon's. I call Bryan and tell him I've had a miscarriage. *Suffered one*, as the doctor said. Bryan is relieved, tells me to come home already.

I can't.

I don't want to.

I hate Bryan Price. I hate that he gave me that ultimatum. He sees the miscarriage as a sign from God. I see it as a mercy, but it hurts anyway. It's what's best for me, but it still breaks me. It wasn't that I was ready to be a mom, per se—I was warming up to the idea. Bryan and I had talked about having kids, but it was not in the five year plan. We were going to settle into our marriage, buy a house. We were broke—I know that. But I'd never expected such a horrible reaction from him. I felt so blindsided by this person I had married—this man with whom I'd just exchanged forever vows.

Overnight, he became someone I didn't know.

And as soon as he ordered me to kill the baby we made, I knew I could never forgive him. I knew I could never sleep next to him, cook dinner for him, let him love me.

Finally, after months of being evasive with my best friend, I break down and tell Robin.

I tell Robin everything.

She's angry. We get an apartment together. Shannon's understanding. Shannon helps me move out and Robin takes me to the library to get books on how to file for divorce. Robin is the one who fields Bryan's angry calls and the time he comes to our door at midnight, screaming, insisting I come home. She encourages me to get a restraining order, but I call Bryan's bluff. He's too proud to do anything to hurt me. He's only hurt I've left, but because I'm silent, I've left the door wide open for Bryan to tell people whatever he wants. He does. He tells our friends and his family that I snapped. I went crazy. I have mental issues. I should be institutionalized.

Of course he never tells anyone I was pregnant.

Of course he never tells anyone he wanted to make me give it up.

Because it's all a bad dream to me, I don't tell anyone else.

Much later, I do tell Paul—after we get engaged. He knows I was married, but at an Italian restaurant, after we talk about wedding venues and whether or not we want a seating chart, I order tiramisu and I open up. I tell Paul everything. He squeezes my hand. He tells me Bryan is a bastard who will get what he has coming one day. I squeeze his hand back.

I don't think often about Bryan or what he put me through, and after Paul and I have our twins—perfectly healthy without a scintilla of complication—I'm so happy, I think about Bryan Price even less.

Time heals all wounds, they say.

Maybe. Time softens the rough edges, like sandpaper. Like erosion. Like the way the incessant beat of the waves in Lake Michigan wear down the shoreline.

Eventually.

Madalynn—*After*

It's my mom who lets the bitch in.

"Someone to see you, Sweetie." She takes Bella. "I'll give this girl a change," she says, and disappears to the nursery, leaving me on my couch, covered in a blanket, no makeup, my hair in a messy bun, face to face with the former Mrs. Price. I'm thankful my mom is staying with me, but I want to be mad at her.

But how could she have known that Kate Barkway is not some friend of mine from work, but someone I would rather never see again my whole life?

Especially like this.

She starts talking before I can say anything.

"Madalynn," she says. I hate her voice. "I won't stay long. I just wanted to give you this."

She hands me a pink gift bag. Tufts of tissue paper poke out. I set it on the coffee table. I don't know if she expects me to open it in front of her, but there is absolutely no way.

"Thanks," I mumble.

"I won't stay long," she repeats. "I just wanted to, you know, give you a little gift. See how the two of you are doing."

I pull the fleece blanket closer to my body. It's nearly Halloween now—getting darker earlier every day. I usually love this time of year—the costumes, the candy, the décor. It's usually all Fall Harvest and pumpkin spice everything. This year, I just want to nestle Bella, get fed by my mom. The last thing I want to do is talk to this lady. I remember how it felt to sucker punch her in the stomach, and the feeling makes me calm.

See how the two of you are doing.

I'm doing well—so Mom tells me. So everyone tells me.

Everyone's so nice. There's a meal train. Gift baskets cover every surface—cards and toys for Bella. I've been surrounded by support from the moment she was born. And—I'm not going to lie, I've got thousands of extra dollars, on top of the life insurance payout—thanks to Stephanie Hoover and the Parks and Recreation Department. I had to take a photograph with Stephanie Hoover, who wanted to bond with me about the baby girl *she* just had.

"We're fine," I say. "You can go." I'm talking quietly in case my mom can hear. I already know I am not going to tell her who this woman is after she leaves, even though my mother will undoubtedly ask in her cheerful way.

I'm hoping Kate will just leave. Instead, she sits across from me—

same place Officer Dorsey sat not too long ago. I think about telling Kate just how big the check was Stephanie gave me, but I figure she already knows.

Just like she knows nothing came from the waiver.

She sent it to me. I forwarded it to my friend, Alexis, who's a lawyer. Alexis very kindly called to tell me I didn't really have a leg to stand on.

Legally, anyway.

What everyone had said all along was true: Bryan had signed a waiver of liability.

That document had released the City of East Grand Rapids Parks and Recreation Department—the race organizers—from responsibility of any negative outcome concerning health, injury, etc. etc. etc.

It was standard, Alexis had said, and there was nothing the race organizers could have done to prevent his death. They had all the proper regulatory practices in place. They had sufficient volunteers. They had sufficient first-aid kits on hand. They'd even had volunteers nearby in the lake in boats, watching the swimmers through binoculars. Two scuba divers lingered below the surface of the water, monitoring the swimmers. Spotters—that's what they called them.

I already knew this. It was one of those scuba divers who had first seen Bryan struggle.

I'd held back tears until I'd hung up the phone with Alexis, then felt all the air whoosh out of me in a clip.

The very next day, I went into labor.

Alexis had told me to let it go—that there was no point pursuing anything further. It would only cost me money and time, both of which were valuable. Especially at this juncture in my life. I heard the words under the words she wasn't saying: I'd been through enough. It was time to let it go.

My mom wanted me to let it go. My dad wanted me to let it go.

One look at Bella's face and I understood why everyone was telling me to let it go.

It had been an accident. It had been no one's fault. It was time to move on. Be thankful. Cherish this beautiful baby girl. She was twenty-one inches long, nearly eight pounds, and absolutely perfect.

Isabella Bryanna Price.

When we were naming her, it was going to be Isabella Rose—Rose for my grandmother. But I knew Bryan would be pleased with this change.

"I'll go," Kate says. "I just—again, just wanted to drop that off.

And I just wanted also to, you know, thank you."

"Thank me?" I don't know what the hell she wants to thank me for.

"The petition," Kate says. "I saw it was rescinded. I wanted to say thank you for that."

"Ah," I say. I did that, too. The other week. Deleted the whole thing. It had gotten up to 102 signatures. It was a silly thing to do, but at the time, it'd made me feel better. Honestly, it was surprising a hundred people agreed with me.

She smiles at me, then, kind of faintly. "You have a beautiful little girl," she says, and thank God, she's standing up now. "Congratulations."

"Thanks," I mutter. I'm happy because she's leaving and I'm happy because I can't think of one reason our paths should ever cross again. I'm trying to stifle the last vestige of anger that she's come here—to my house—that she knows where I live. But I've been doing that for weeks now—tamping down my anger.

That it happened.

That she was in charge of that race. That she'd been the one who made the decision to deny him that fucking snorkel. She could have just said sure—*it's fine. Who cares?*

But she didn't.

I knew it was time to let it go, just as I'd let go of the idea that I could sue her or the city. Didn't matter. It wouldn't bring Bryan back. Plus, I made more from the proceeds of the race than I ever would have made from a lawsuit.

Maybe, anyway.

"Well thanks," I say to her backside. My mom can hear that. She'll probably tell me it would have been better manners to walk my guest to the door, but I'm banking on her giving me a pass.

But she turns then—Kate does—and gives me this very weird smile.

"I wish you all the best, Madalynn," she says. "You take good care of her, and yourself."

I make a face, but she doesn't see it. She's already turned to leave. Once I hear the door close behind her, I yell for Mom to bring me back my baby girl.

Kate—*Before*

Standing by the registration table, collecting the leftover bibs, I felt the slight breeze on my skin, the heavy haze of the hangover in my brain.

I fought the strong desire to go back to sleep, or to swim in a pool of coffee. The day felt thin and overwhelming. I know it wasn't Stephanie's fault she got pregnant and had to miss today, but I was suddenly so resentful she'd forced me into her shoes.

I didn't want to do this. I should still be warm in my bed, asleep next to Paul.

The static of the walkie-talkie brought me back to the moment. Chelsea's question crackled on the other end.

"Hey, Kate," Chelsea said. She's using her uber-professional tone. It's different from the tone she uses when it's just the two of us in the break room. "I've got a swimmer here with a snorkel. Bill wasn't sure—he thought maybe they weren't allowed. The athlete's about to go in."

Again, the silence, the heavy dull dread of my own brain.

I searched my tired, hungover brain.

For the life of me, I cannot remember encountering anything about snorkels in all the reading I'd done in the pages of Stephanie's well-organized binder. There'd been a section about race gear, but I couldn't remember anything about snorkels.

But was I wrong? Or just hungover? Was Bill right? Wouldn't he know?

I couldn't think. My whole head was in a vice, and someone somewhere was gradually tightening the lever. I couldn't think and I couldn't remember. I couldn't begin to imagine the right answer. *I should just trust Bill*, I thought. *Why argue with Bill?*

Then, I tried something else: I tried to picture the photos hanging around the Parks and Recreation Office. I imagined all the large posters of proud triathletes of the past. Strong men and women in wetsuits coming out of the water of Reeds Lake; confident cyclists; runners approaching the finishing line with million-dollar smiles.

Nowhere in my memory could I locate a photo of a swimmer with a snorkel.

Goggles, sure—fogged up and wet.

Wet suits, uncomfortably tight. Showing every curve of the body. I would never don a wetsuit—at least not at my current weight.

Maybe if I ever successfully lost the forty pounds I'd been trying to lose since Kevin and Krista were toddlers…

"Kate?"

"I'm here."

I could Google it. A quick search might give me an answer. But as I reached into my pocket, I realized my cell wasn't there.

I left my cell in my purse. I left my purse in my car.

Damn hangover. *Dammit, Paul.*

"What should we do, boss? The starting gun's about to go off for this wave."

It was Chelsea again. I imagined her getting a little impatient. Perhaps Chelsea wished she had just answered the swimmer's question. She regrets having involved me.

Ask for forgiveness, not permission—wasn't that the saying?

Chelsea could have just said yes to Bill and never asked the Interim Director.

But Chelsea was an *ask permission, not forgiveness* kind of person. Then Chelsea said, quite unmistakably, "Racer 279 is anxious for an answer!"

Racer 279.

A flash ripped through my brain like lightening.

Triathletes 30, 224, 17, 83, 90, and 192 neglected to pick up their packets this morning; small disasters or crises of confidence had kept them from starting the race they had signed up and paid for.

I couldn't attach any names to those racers.

If a gun were to my head, I knew I couldn't name a single other racer on that registration list Chelsea printed out, but I knew who Racer 279 was.

I knew he wasn't a strong swimmer—that when he was young, he didn't exercise. He used to make fun of people in spandex. He used to say he would only run if a bear were chasing him. He used to smoke a pack a day. In fact, he had exercise-induced asthma. He was so embarrassed the doctor had given him an inhaler for it, he'd made me promise not to tell anyone.

That vacation in the Keys… he'd not gone into the water once. Unless dipping his toes in the hotel's hot tub counted. It was odd, really. I'd never met anyone so scared of deep water.

"I'm sorry," I said into the walkie-talkie. "Bill's right. Snorkels are not permitted. Thanks for checking. I'll be down in a minute."

I turned the walkie-talkie off before Chelsea could respond.

Before anyone had anything else to say.

Best of luck to you, Racer 279, I thought. *Sounds like you could use a little extra help. That you wish you had just a little more support. Hmm.*

It's hard, huh? Having the wind knocked out of your sails like that. Not being able to depend on something you thought you could.

Then I smiled.

Then, I started walking to the shoreline, toward the throng of eager, ready racers.

I couldn't wait to see how this ended.

Author's Note

Thank you to my writing critique group who read sections of this novella: Norman Belanger, Garrett Stack, and Megan Turner. I owe Megan in particular a debt of gratitude for helping me finalize editorial decisions and for writing such kind words about this novella.

Thank you to Bob Johnson for your thoughtful endorsement as well!

Thank you, Marc J. Sheehan, for lending me a line from your story, "The Sad Decline of the Side-show." The story is contained in Marc's excellent collection, *Dissenting Opinion from the Committee for the Beatitudes* (Etchings Press, 2019).

The novella's cover comes from the very talented West Michigan artist Ben Boss; Ben, thank you for trusting me with *The Unmooring*. It is the perfect cover for this wicked little tale.

Thank you to the folks at Regal House Publishing who honored an earlier version of this novella by longlisting it for *The Fugere Book Prize for Finely Crafted Novellas* (2023).

And thank you to Leah Maines and the family at Finishing Line Press for bringing this novella into the world.

The final thank you goes to my family—in particular my husband Micah, who never hesitates to tell me I can do hard things (or disappear with my laptop whenever I need to).

Colleen Alles is a writer, former librarian & teacher, and Michigan girl for life. She earned her bachelor's degree in English from Michigan State University (2005) and her MLIS from Wayne State University (2015). Her fiction and poetry have appeared in *Red Cedar Review*, *Tar River Poetry*, *The Write Michigan Anthology*, *The Michigan Poet*, and other places. Colleen is co-editor for fiction with *Barren Magazine* and is currently pursuing her MFA in poetry at Spalding University (Louisville, KY). Her most recent book of poetry was recently a finalist for the Woodrow Hall Top Shelf Award. This is her second novella. Colleen is represented by Jenna Satterthwaite (Storm Literary Agency). Colleen writes, runs, reads, and worries she wouldn't make sense outside the Midwest.

www.ingramcontent.com/pod-product-compliance
Lightning Source LLC
LaVergne TN
LVHW090536110826
845146LV00003B/1131